T0288550

# Praise for Jim Krueger

"Jim Krueger is one of the best writers there is."
–*Sam Raimi*; Director, *EVIL DEAD* series, *SPIDER-MAN* and many global cinema hits.

"As a consummate storyteller, Jim Krueger cajoles and conjures, shocks and soothes, glides and guides, and the reader can just sit back and get swept away. Jim's life is story, and that is clear with every word on the page."
–*Todd Komarnicki*, Novelist; Producer of the Christmas blockbuster, *ELF*; and screenwriter of such hits as SULLY.

"This collection of charmingly strange Yuletide treasures showcases Jim's uncanny ability to take stories and themes we thought we knew and completely redefine them, injecting them with heart, depth, and more than a little darkness. The tales contained herein will plunge you deep into the unexplored corners of the Christmas season."
–*Patrick McHale*, the creator of *OVER THE GARDEN WALL* animated series, and writer of Del Toro's *PINOCCHIO*.

O' Haunted Night
Book 1

# The Frankincense Monster and Other Creepy Christmas Stories

By
Jim Krueger

13 Stories

The Frankincense Monster and
Other Creepy Christmas Stories

All Rights Reserved

ISBN-13: 978-1-922856-90-6

IFWG Publishing International
Gold Coast
www.ifwgpublishing.com

# Table of Contents

# Introduction

There's something creepy about Christmas.

Bear with me for a sec, I'll explain.

When you think about the season of Christmas—early winter, it's just after the solstice, close enough to the shortest day of the year to be acutely aware of the long, long nights. It's cold in most places. Houses are shut up. Fires are alight in some homes, or low lights are burning. Family and friends tend to reach out, to visit, to catch up on everything that's happened over the last year. It's time to take stock of new births and sad deaths, marriages and divorces, joy and heartache. It's also close to the death of the year that has been and the almost—but not quite—fresh start to a new year.

There's a lot going on.

For those with deeply-felt religious beliefs, it's a time to celebrate. Not only Christmas, but Hanukkah, Kwanzaa, Bodhi Day, Yule, and others. Yes, even Festivus.

Since Christmas is, by definition a Christian holiday, it's built on the bones of older celebrations from cultures, such as Rome's Saturnalia, that have largely faded. The echoes are there—the decorated tree, fairy lights, gift-giving, stockings hung by the fire, caroling, decking the halls with holly—and all have their roots in pagan festivals. So there is that sense of antiquity and of things gone but not quite forgotten. There are, in point of fact, *ghosts* of old traditions that haunt our current celebrations.

When folks gathered on cold, dark nights, storytelling was important. Some of the stories told are family tales, apocryphal anecdotes of past deeds, tall tales, and some classic yarns about days gone by. Implicit in any 'old story' is a subconscious awareness that we are talking about people who have since died.

Some tales told around the family hearth or around a camp-fire in some lonely place—cowpokes huddled against the cold on the long winter nights in the canyons, hunters, soldiers, travelers—were spooky. Those tales are fun to tell on a winter's night. Everyone is home because of the weather, and that creates a captive audience. The knowledge—and, again, often unconscious—that leaving is not really an option, creates the right atmosphere for being a bit scared.

This tradition changed somewhat over the last couple of hundred years. Oral storytelling was largely replaced by books that were mass-produced and widely distributed during the Victorian era. Reading became encouraged, and so people began reading books. Novels and short stories flourished during this time. And it was in this era that homes slowly changed from those warmed by fires and lit by candles to having gas heat and electric lights. People would seek out their favorite room, favorite chair, and read in solitude. Kids would do that with flashlights under the blankets as the winter winds made bare tree branches scratch suspiciously at the windows.

But radio brought the family back together again, and radio dramas were as often filled with spooky tales as they were with news and dramas.

One perennial favorite that was told around fireplaces, read in solitary bedrooms or studies, and dramatized on the radio was *A Christmas Carol*.

Most folks remember it for the generosity and joy that Scrooge brought on Christmas Day, but most of what came before that was some rough stuff. The book is worth re-reading if you haven't read it lately. I read it every year, and I listen to it on audio, and watch many of the film and TV adaptations. Two of the latter stand out for me—the George C. Scott/David Warner version, which was subtle, sophisticated, and disturbing, with perhaps the quintessential Ghost of Marley in the person of Frank Finlay; and the more recent and decidedly *not* family friendly *A Christmas Carol* starring Guy Pearce. The latter is scary, disturbing, appalling, offensive, and very well done. It takes the core themes of Dickens' classic tale and twists them until they bleed. Quite nasty at times, and with a payoff that does not redeem Scrooge at all.

Charles Dickens' short novel is one of the best ghost stories ever written. It stands up to the passage of time because the themes within it are universal—greed, empathy and antipathy, generosity, want, privation, joy, and redemption. It is the book I have read more than any other, though the other books that flesh out my five yearly reads are, as you'll note, hewn closer to the spookier themes in *A Christmas Carol* than the celebratory ones. They are *The Haunting of Hill House* by Shirley Jackson; *I Am Legend* by Richard Matheson; *The Halloween Tree* by Ray Bradbury; and the *Collected Ghost Stories* of M.R. James.

All spooky.

All dealing, in one way or another with isolation, fear, the unknown, and the weird. They are, in fact, my emotional support books. I find comfort in their familiarity; I rely on the sense of balance in each, because in one way or another the inexplicable will become known, though the core mysteries might not be satisfactorily resolved.

I like my winter nights dark, and I like my tales weird, strange, unnerving, and disturbing, but with little bits of lightness and humor.

Which brings me to *this* book you're currently holding.

Jim Krueger is as much a Christmas nut as I am. Possibly more so. Like me, he enjoys the storytelling potential of such an important holiday, and likes to have some fun playing with the model. This volume of Christmas tales is *not* likely to be told to little kids around the fire. Or, maybe they will, if the kids are anything like I was. Kids who not only don't mind being scared, but seek out that kind of experience.

They're also intended for people who don't take anything—even their own fears—too seriously. Some of these are laugh out loud. Others are touching. All of them are weird.

What shines through the stories, no matter how light or dark the themes, is Jim's sense of fun. Fun does not always mean nicely-wrapped presents and a new puppy. What is fun for us—and I suspect for you since you bought this book—is not necessarily fun for those with weaker nerves. I enjoy dark tales well told. I love stories that push me out of my comfort zone. And I really adore stories that surprise me.

The stories here did all of that.

These are oddball tales. Christmas stories, sure, but with mummies, cannibals, bad kids, bad adults, strange creatures, and even vampires.

Ho…ho…uh-oh…?

Yeah.

Fun stuff. The kind of entertaining tales that let me know the writer had someone like me in mind—someone off-kilter and willing to step into the dark without a reliable flashlight.

It's hard to pick a favorite, and I won't even try. When I discover a new batch of short stories, I often go back and re-read early ones once I've become familiar with the scope and range of the writer. That's why I revisit M.R. James—his stories are different to me as an adult and as a professional writer than they were when I first read them as an eleven-year-old living in poverty in the inner city. I suspect these stories will have a similar draw for me, and there are some I know for sure I'll come back to again and again.

So, my fellow holiday weirdo…put another log on the fire, turn the Christmas music down to a murmur, pour yourself a tall cup of holiday cheer, and turn the page.

And enjoy!


Jonathan Maberry
San Diego, June 2024

# Out Of The Box

## An Author's Justification at Christmas

The stories you are about to read are original amalgamations of the symbols and images of both the traditional Christmas stories and those themes considered more modern and well, elfish. These are the first thirteen of what I hope to be an advent calendar of holiday horror. A story a day. A door to be opened to a new room every day in this haunted holiday house.

That said, I'll let you supply your own chocolate. Some like bitter, some like sweet. But you will find both in these pages. That is, the bitter and the sweet. The sad and the hopeful. The merry and the scary.

They're ghost stories, yes. But beware, monsters are also mulling around, if only to spice things up. Most are meant for the whole family to enjoy. Some you may not want to tell your parents about, no matter how old they are.

Christmas to me is about things that don't quite add up, and I'm not speaking about debt, that always adds up this time of year.

No, it's about giant things fitting into impossible spaces. About love being found in a box. Hope being stuffed elegantly into an envelope. About certain destinies being changed in the giving of an engagement ring. It's even about a big, jolly, fat guy fitting into the tiniest of chimneys.

It can also be a sad and poignant time. But one that lasts only until the promise of a New Year and a new beginning that can then be written.

What I'm about to tell you is clearly not the way to introduce a Christmas book, but...Because it was the appropriate time to do so, I told my daughter a short time ago that there was no Santa Claus. I said that Santa was a disguise parents use to give presents in secret because there's no better way to give a gift than in secret.

She told me she still wanted to believe. I said he wasn't real, and it didn't matter to her at all.

If anything, that is the message of Christmas. Of the very rebelliousness of the time. The things everyone says and knows cannot possibly be real, *are*. Myths become real, as if by a miracle.

Some things are too large for the little rules that rule our lives.

They're too big for any box.

Yet, there they are.

Even under one cover.

Peace.

Jim Krueger

# DENIED BEFORE CHRISTMAS

Christmas sucks. And believe me, I know an awful lot about sucking. I'm a vampire. Yeah, one of the legions of the undead.

I was bitten when I was seventeen years old.

I thought she was just giving me a hickey.

But I also figured it would be no big deal. I like to sleep in as it is. In fact, I thought that I had gotten lucky (and I had. It's me, remember). I remember thinking that now I'm forever young. I'm an eternal babe-magnet even without the hypnotic vision. And I will drink life to the full, forever.

At least, that's what they tell you right after they bite you. But, now that I think about it, I think that's one of those things that's actually an apology. They say you'll drink life to the fullest, but there's a sort of sadness to it at the same time. Because shortly after you experience this new life, this summer of opportunity, something changes. Summer turns into fall, which becomes December. And the hours between feedings are always cold.

You'd think that being an immortal would leave you nothing to fear. You'd think it would be everything you've always dreamed of. But it isn't.

For example, there is almost no place safe on Earth to be a vampire on Christmas.

Most vampires go north to Alaska, where it can be night this time of year for a long, long time. Or some of us delve deep into the shadows of the Grand Canyon, or hang in dormant volcanoes, or any such thing this time of year. I've even heard tell of underwater vampires, where the sun never shines. But really, who wants to be wet all the time. And while fish blood *is* technically blood, it is kind of fishy. So; no to the big blue.

Basically, getting away from people, and almost all people, is the goal.

And that's because no vampire is safe, not a one of us. Somehow this 'Spirit of Christmas' infects everybody. It's like a disease, or a plague, or maybe even a curse.

We usually feed on lower animals this time of year, in fear of infection. It's not really the healthiest of diets, but nothing tastes worse than the blood of someone who has Christmas in his or her heart.

I can't tell you how grateful I am that people don't celebrate it every day, how thankful I am that most get the whole 'peace on Earth' and 'good will to men' thing out of their system by the New Year. I mean, where would we be if everyone acted that kind and considerate every day of the year?

Many people don't know this, but there is a sort of mentor program in the league of the undead. New vampires are brought in, trained in who and what makes a proper victim, how to spot virgins (not that I ever had a problem with that), how to recognize a vampire hunter and other survival techniques. An old vampire hunter named Gunter trained me. Of course, he wasn't a vampire hunter any more.

But after a while, after all the training and mentoring, you just…well, you just want to try to do things your own way. Gunter said I felt this way because although I was forever a stud (not his words), I was forever a teenager and pain in the ass (his words). And psychologically would forever be a rebel. He said it like it was a bad thing. Can I help it if Gunter was bitten when he was already in his sixties? Already old?

Anyhow, one year I decided I wasn't going to do what my

vampire brothers and sisters do every year. I decided I was going to stay home in New York City. Some say the people in NYC are the hardest, most sarcastic in the world. So I thought I had nothing to fear.

It was Christmas Eve when I walked into Rosie's Bar to hang out. Rosie's was the kind of place where the police should have gone when they were looking for criminals. Except, of course, they're too afraid. It was the place all the scumbags of the world went to get lost and not get found. It was hard and mean and fights were fought there almost nightly.

And you know what I found when I went there that Christmas Eve? You're not going to believe it. Grown felons were singing Christmas songs. Men who would normally cut your throat-and I've always been on the best terms with their kind-were helping each other and hugging and crying together. Drunks who never muttered anything in any language apart from indistinguishable slurs were now spitting and hiccupping the words to '*Silent Night*'. Some of the regulars there—you know, the usual suspects—were even saying things like, and I hate to mention it, but they said things like "I'm sorry," and "Can you forgive me?"

Grown men. Men hardened by years of murder and lies and cheating, suddenly finding they still had a conscience? You can see some pretty terrible things in New York, but this was the worst.

I could find nothing to drink in the bar at all.

The next place I visited was down on Wall Street. Those that work here are not unlike the undead; they feed upon their fellow men for personal advancement.

And you know what I saw? They were feeding the homeless and they were giving their money away. Many lit candles to remember lost family members and say prayers. Some were still up late doing legal work for those that couldn't afford their services. Them, those white-collar yuppies (I was bitten in the 80's, a wonderful time), and believe me, we do notice collars. Anyhow, the white collars were helping others without considering the cost.

So where can you go when even the rich betray you?

I had an idea.

I flew up to Queens after this, looking for the poor.

But even there I found a similar, if not even more sickening, behavior. Families that might have lifted guns against each other were instead opening their homes up to each other. They were worse than the rich were. They shared out of having nothing. And their neighbors were overwhelmed with gifts that were almost less than nothing.

What really made me sick was how many times I heard these people saying the same thing: "We should do this more often."

"Why do we only think of each other one time a year? We should do this all the time," they said.

Some even said, "Let me see if I can help again once the holidays are over."

You'd think they'd have the decency, if they have to say things like that, to limit it to this time of year.

I cannot fully describe the horror that had come upon me. Surely here, in New York, people would be different. I mean, this was boring. It was the same thing over and over and over again.

Most people know how we vampires feel about religious symbols. Well, a Christmas tree isn't much different than a cross when it comes down to it.

And the idea of everyone talking about peace lasting forever and ever and living forever in the spirit of love and charity…well it feels sort of blasphemous to my kind. It's not very sensitive to the undead, you know?

In other words, it's just not woke for those who don't walk during the day, okay?

No one should have that sort of hope in light of other people who come from other walks of life.

I searched the city well into the night. And turned up nothing. All people regardless of health and circumstance were the same pathetic type that night.

My mentor was right. Screw old people. This is no place for

someone like me. I can't make it in New York on Christmas. And that means I can't make it anywhere.

I flew north, leaving the city and the lights behind me, and finally after finding nowhere that I would feel welcome, I discovered in the darkness an old farm and some stables.

The thought of not finding anywhere to stay except a stable, and the sound and stink of the animals that lived in the barn, made me remember the Christmas nativity story, which gave me a terrible headache and caused my ears to smoke.

Christmas sucks.

'Course, even without the company of family and friends, I still had one of the best ham dinners of my life.

Well, afterlife, at least.

# COAL

Mary Crow was born into a family of monsters. And the Crows were the worst kind of monsters because they were human. For your information, human monsters are different to almost any other kind of monster because they don't look like monsters. And it can take a long time to get the hint that there's something dark and scary and just plain wrong about them, something in the depths that is very black indeed.

And worse, this darkness may be almost impossible to get out of a person once it's there.

The Crow family was filthy rich with an emphasis on filthy. They owned a coal mine. They owned the mountain the coal mine was established upon. And that meant they also owned the town and all the people just below the mountain that depended on the jobs in the mine.

For those that don't know, coal is a type of rock that can make things that are very cold very warm. Except, ironically and emotionally speaking, of course, in the case of the Crow family itself. They were just cold no matter what.

There was nothing wrong with young Mary Crow, though. She was kind and thoughtful and saw the good in people even though there was nothing good to see in her immediate family.

Perhaps that was even the reason why the good in people, no matter how small, was so easy for her to spot. She had spent so long searching for it in her own family.

Mary spent her days shoveling coal into the furnace to warm the manor. More than four hundred men worked the mines at any time, and many of them lived in the manor until there was a holiday or they had some time off to go and visit their families in the valley. So, the job of keeping them all warm was a big one. And Mary had to shovel enough coal to warm the entire manor for the entire night.

Mary had just turned seventeen. But this had been her job since she was eleven.

To give you an idea of just how bad her family was, she had been offered in marriage to whichever worker broke the record for coal hauling, regardless of their age, weight, stink or disposition.

Mary dreamed of marriage; yes, she dreamed of princes and magic kingdoms as so many girls do.

But this was a nightmare.

Many of the workers came to her while she was shoveling coal into the furnace to tell her that they were going to win her. She'd smile, because that was her nature. But none of these workers were sweet. None valued kindness. And each one that came to win her was only interested in getting her by picking coal, not by finding her heart.

When her father and mother saw her frustration, although she tried to hide it, they began locking her in the attic at night, in fear that she might run away. Her door would then be unlocked every morning when it was time to stoke and load the furnaces again.

She really had nothing to hope for, except for one thing, something small in light of everything else. Still, it made all the bad stuff in her life seem a little less real.

Christmas was coming.

**B**ut first, there is something to understand about stories. Inside of every story, there are a lot of other little stories, like little gems all glistening along the way. These little characteristics add flavor and depth and irony to a story.

Such moments appear even here, in this terrible, loathsome tale about the Crow family, although who would expect to find gems in a coal mine, really?

For the sake of this story though, you need to understand that the Crow's coal mine was not all that was going on in the world, especially since Christmas was coming.

This was all happening at a time when the person known as Santa Claus had just begun bringing gifts to people and was learning how to use magic to make his job easier. This was all happening before Santa started considering going global with his gift-giving, when his efforts were really based in Europe.

It was also a time before his love for milk and cookies got the better of his waistline. *(But that's already too much said about a very delicate issue for the Santa we all know today. Let's just say he's working on it and get back to the Santa of Mary Crow's time.)*

Santa was already growing elves at the North Pole, where the ice is best for growing toy-making elves. For anyone who's wondered why elves have green skin, it's because they are more like plants than people. For those that find this hard to believe, in regards to elves; you can see something almost fern-like if you look closely at the curl and pointedness of their ears.

It was a lonesome job that Santa had at the North Pole. And it was hard to water the elves because the water freezes almost instantly and would often hit them in the head instead of helping them grow. This may explain for some why all elves are so short, but who can be certain?

Santa had also begun to teach reindeer how to fly. He hoped to fly to his destinations by sleigh, and to not spend almost all of December bringing gifts to people. He had this world-changing idea that by using magic and this sleigh, he could do it all in one night. He had not yet tested the deer or the sleigh.

This year, like those few years past, he would begin distributing gifts the night of December 5th which, to this day, is still known, especially in Europe, as Saint Nicholas' Night. They called him a saint because many believed him to be so kind, and so nice, that he had to be a saint of some sort.

He had also learned how to watch people all over Europe by coloring the winds and the air that blew to the North with a magic paintbrush. The paintbrush was a gift from some very artistic witches who were very thankful for the dollhouses he had made for them, not to mention certain gardening tips. He used the paintbrush to discover what people wanted during the holidays. And what exactly he could have the elves build for people.

This was a time before the masses talked about him having a nice and naughty list. This was a time when he brought gifts for everyone on the planet.

Santa, as he had done the year before, began preparing the toys and gifts for those that lived on Crow Mountain. He had decided to visit there on the night of December 24th. He took a brush to the winds, and noticed something very peculiar about the Crow family. The Crows didn't want him to come to their mountain at all. They were very upset that the workers had received anything from anyone else the year before. Beauregarde Crow, or Pa Crow as his family called him, felt these gifts made the workers lazy and lethargic knowing they would get a gift they didn't have to work for; or worse than that, a gift that they didn't have to thank the Crow family for.

Worse, it gave the workers a chance to leave the manor and go down into the valley for a day to spend time with their own families.

The Crows hated the idea that on the 26th of December, the workers would be that much later for work, or at least warmed and made lazy by the comforts of their own wives and children and brothers and daughters.

Santa noticed that the Crows were preparing for his coming by setting traps. They were making snares whose very purpose was to let Santa know that he was not welcome on Crow Mountain.

And if, perhaps, Santa lost a toe or two in the process… well, that would just keep him from getting any ideas in the many years ahead.

So Santa knew of their traps and plans. Yes, he did. And it's not unfair to think of Santa wondering if he should even go to Crow Mountain at all. But Santa had also become aware of something else; *someone* else. He had seen Mary for the very first time. Perhaps it was because she had been locked in the attic and there wasn't really any way for the air in the attic to reach the North Pole. Or maybe it was because, like everyone else in the manor, she was so covered in soot so much of the time, that he just never took note of her.

The important thing was, though, that he saw her now.

He was amazed that even in the midst of so terrible a family, there was someone so kind and so good and so wonderful as Mary.

He saw that she was very upset about the plans to hurt him. He had been her hope. And Santa realized that the coming attack on him was also an attempt to quell her hope.

Mary had been willing to suffer her family *because* it was her family, and to some extent she felt she owed them her life. But the idea of their terrible Christmas wishes being put upon someone who was so good, who only gave and tried to make the world better…well, this was too much to bear. It broke her heart. And Santa saw this broken heart as well.

Her family also saw this. And unfortunately, they couldn't have been happier. They never approved of her good nature or the way she made the best of situations that would have been perfectly fine to just accept as deplorable. They felt it was downright rebellious on her part.

But they also considered the possibility that after Santa was put in his place, she would welcome all their efforts to find her a husband.

Santa was, of course, troubled. After looking deeply into her broken heart, he asked the elves to make a new one for her.

After much work, they showed him one that was guaranteed not to break, and came with batteries that would last a minimum of one hundred and fifty years. But Santa was not satisfied. The heart itself was flawless and would have made Mary stronger, yes, but he feared the kindness and compassion she had showed would now be missing as well. The elves went back to the workshop. But the more they worked, and the more prototypes they constructed, the more something became obvious to Santa-that magical elves can't build everything.

Even in Santa's toy factory, even there, there were limits.

After Mary's heart broke, the Crows stopped locking Mary in the attic. All of them could see that with her broken heart, there was no danger of her running away. Pa Crow thought it would even make her a better wife for whichever worker was lucky enough to increase the year's quota.

But she continued in her work, loading coal, and more coal into the furnace. At night, when everyone else had gone to sleep, she would sit in front of the Christmas tree with a faraway look on her face. As if she were hoping to be reminded of something.

*Don't be confused by the Christmas tree.* The Crow family didn't celebrate the holidays, even in their own way. It was part of the trap set for Santa. *And Mary knew the tree now meant death.* Death for Santa.

On Christmas Eve, the family gathered in front of their fireplace and all drank an alcoholic concoction that was very bitter and so thick that it was almost chewy. They joked that it was like mother's milk to them, which might offer an explanation as to why they were all so terrible. And where, perhaps, they actually came from.

The Crows celebrated that this would be the last year they'd have to deal with Santa and his bothersome and very selfish agenda of giving gifts to perfect strangers.

One of Mary's many brothers laughed at her and told her that after this, once Santa saw them as his master, that all Santa would be bringing her would be more coal for her to shovel; and Pa Crow had a mean old belly laugh at this joke. The others not only laughed but cheered. And after they had all gotten suitably drunk and stupid, they struggled, staggered and slouched their way to their beds, leaving Mary under the lethal Christmas tree.

Here's how the traps worked. All the doors and windows in the manor had been locked to make certain Santa could not enter in any other way than through the chimney: The trick needed him to come down that way. And when, at last, his boots hit bottom, the Crows had rigged the floor and wood in the fireplace to ignite, thus giving Santa a scorched welcome. They joked that this would give him a taste of the South Pole (and given that the South Pole is just as cold as the North, it was a very feeble and ignorant attempt at a joke).

After falling, while aflame, into the main room of the house, and trying to douse the fires on his boots, they had rigged the Christmas Tree to fall on Santa. They had also intentionally never watered the tree, so that the needles would be quite dry and would scratch him terribly. The tree, catching fire on Santa's boots, would finish the job for them. These terrible people were expecting the smell of barbeque the next morning.

Yes, barbeque.

They really were monsters.

Mary's heart was broken, yes, but that did not mean that she was incapable of any acts of kindness. She had been waiting for Santa, waiting to warn him of what her family was doing. And it took all her strength to just wait and try to help. But she was also so tired. Tired of it all. Maybe it would a miracle if she'd be able to warn him. But that might be enough.

Santa's sleigh finally pulled up in front of the manor. And, finding all the doors locked, Santa proceeded to the chimney. This was the first chimney Santa would ever climb down, but he was now so accustomed to magic and its many old and ancient uses, that the chimney was not a problem for him to squeeze through.

And of course, Santa knew the trap that had been set for him. Once again he was tempted not to visit the Crows at all. But that would mean that Mary and the families of the miners would go without Christmas gifts. It would mean that the Crows had won.

He knew he had to come, if only to give Mary the heart he had finally found for her.

Santa positioned himself above the chimney and shook his boots. The ice from the North Pole flaked down, all the way into the trap that had been set. By the time Santa reached the bottom of the fireplace, the trap was too soggy to ignite in any way.

He stepped out of the fireplace, and looked at the tree. It was even drier than he had anticipated. He nodded and with a little magic taken from what he knew about growing elves, he watered it, making it greener and healthier than the day it was first cut down.

He distributed the presents he had brought with him and finally turned to Mary, who was asleep. She was so kind and beautiful. She shouldn't be here. He took a small piece of coal from his bag and put it in her hand. He knew she'd understand.

And then he left. He had many more presents to give. And many more people to visit.

When Mary woke and opened her eyes the next morning and saw the present Santa had left for her, she smiled. It warmed her in ways no one could imagine. She wished she could have seen him. But of course, this was now December 25th, and there were other children, other presents and places for him to visit.

When the Crow family woke up, despite feeling terribly hung over from the night before, they raced down to see the carnage their traps had caused for Santa.

They did not expect to find the tree still standing, or smelling the way perfect Christmas trees do, or looking as perfect as it did. They also did not expect to hear Mary humming to herself and smiling again. They did not expect to find so many presents waiting for them from the person they had tried so literally to burn.

Now, for some this would be a miracle enough. It would melt the coldness in a person's heart. It would make them see the warmth of human kindness and the beauty of grace and charity.

But not the Crows.

They were angry, even angrier than they had been the year before. And worse, Mary's broken heart seemed to be whole once again.

One of Mary's brothers asked what Santa had brought her.

She smiled. "You were right. He brought me a piece of coal."

Her brother laughed and joked that maybe this Santa

wasn't all bad. But they all knew that he was. He was terrible.

Regardless, Ma and Pa Crow saw that their daughter was changed. They saw that she would not settle for the life they had chosen for her.

And that evening she was locked in the attic again. But it did no good at all.

The next morning they found that she was gone. There was a hole in the roof, although no one understood how it had gotten there.

The workers in the Crow Mines eventually became frustrated with the working conditions and found new ways to make a living for themselves by serving each other's needs alongside their own families. Having run out of coal and people to dig it, the Crows eventually sold the mountain and left for a warmer climate.

After a while, almost no one even ventured up into Crow Mountain.

As for Mary, well, no one ever saw her again. Some said she had died. Others said she had run away, not willing to be won as a bride. And many tell ghost stories and suggest she might still be up there on the mountain shoveling coal when the winds sound like the screams and rantings of the Crows.

But none of these stories are true. Mary had been locked in the attic. But she wasn't upset about being alone up there. She knew he was coming for her. Christmas was over. And now he could be concerned with more than just giving to everyone he was aware of.

Now Santa could be concerned for just her.

She heard the bells jingling moments before she heard the tiny footsteps of deer on the roof above her head.

She heard a sawing that sounded not much different than Pa Crow snoring. And then part of the roof fell in and a black gloved hand reached down to pull her up out of the attic, out of Crow Manor, out of the life she had, out of the soot and ash.

Santa had come for her.

He asked if she was ready.

She was.

She asked if he was certain.

He was.

Her heart had been broken, and there was no building or constructing or inventing a new one.

It was broken, and so there was only one thing to do when it comes to hearts. She needed a new one. And, so, he gave her…

…his.

You might think of this as the story of how Santa got a wife. And you would be right. But perhaps it's the story of the first time Santa used his flying sleigh. Or went down a chimney. And maybe it's about the one time in the history of the world that Santa actually brought coal to someone.

For Mary did receive coal that Christmas morning. It was a small and compressed piece of coal at that. But as far as diamonds and engagement rings go, it was one of the biggest imaginable.

All stories are full of such gems.

# RAIN DEER

We have all heard stories of how cruel reindeer can be. We have all listened to the tales of their exclusive games and of their wanton snootiness. Yet they are also the means by which so many gifts are brought to children around the world. So perhaps we should not judge them too harshly. And they, like all of us, have much to learn.

It was a cruel name to call her. Her real name was Donna. Not Donner. Donna. And what they called her was downright nasty, actually. At first she didn't understand the joke, or why they all laughed.

They saw that she didn't understand and giggled all the more at what they perceived as her dullness in comprehension. And then, because they had meant the joke to hurt, and were all so full of their own cleverness, they explained themselves.

"We weren't calling you 'Reindeer' because you are just like us. We were calling you 'Rain deer' because you're nothing like us. You can't fly."

And then they flew off, leaving Donna alone and sad in the forest where they had all been playing. Gravity isn't just for objects. It can refer to words as well. And these carried a terrible weight to them.

She watched them go. And was glad to know, at least, that they were not her friends. She had suspected, but now she knew this for certain. The not knowing was always worse than the knowing.

She could run, though—faster than any other reindeer. And she prided herself on how much higher than all of them she could jump, while reminding herself at the same time that jumping was not considered much of a talent by those who could fly.

Were they really all so different? She had four legs just like they did. Her fur was brown and soft just like theirs.

But unlike them, she couldn't stay aloft.

Her parents told her she couldn't fly because she was afraid, and maybe she was. But not of flying. She would never be afraid of flying. She longed for flight with every hair of her coat. She dreamed of escaping the cruelty of gravity.

No. She was afraid of the others. She was afraid of their words. Of the words they said to her face and even the words she couldn't hear them say but she knew they said. And what, what if she could actually fly but wasn't a good enough flier? What if they laughed at the way she flew? Or she couldn't fly as fast? What then?

The days before Christmas Eve were the worst days of the year for her. This was the time of the Sleigh Games. For little Donna, the deer that couldn't fly, this was pure torture. How she hated Christmas. Not because she didn't like gifts, but because she felt that this day, more than any other day, was the one time during the year that she didn't have anything to give. She had nothing to offer.

It was so terrible, in fact, that every Christmas, she just wanted to die.

Tabby, another reindeer who everyone thought would be the first female to join Santa's sleigh-team, was the worst. When Tabby said that Donna should run away and join the zoo, she placed heavy emphasis on "run". At least in a zoo, no one would know about her. No one would know how far, in terms of North Pole reindeer, she had fallen.

But not everything in Donna's life was awful. Donna had a little brother. She had someone to love and who loved her back. Donna's brother's name was Rudolph; Rudy.

Rudy, who was much younger than Donna, could fly... well, fly most of the time. When he was cold, or he got scared, he did have some trouble, though. Rudy, who was friends with almost everybody (though he had his own issue that, at this point of his life, he kept a disguised secret), never told anyone but Donna about his fear. This was *their* secret. And their secret alone.

Rudy made Donna promise to never tell anyone.

"Donna?"

"Yes, Rudy?"

"My friends. They say awful things about you."

"I know," she admitted.

"They're not really my friends, then, are they? I mean, if they knew about my, you know, they would..."

"No...I don't know. Maybe they are your friends. They're just not my friends, that's for certain." Donna waited a moment. Was it right for her to say that they couldn't be Rudy's friends? And what would they do if Rudy's other issue were ever to become known to the greater world of reindeer?

"Do you care?" her brother asked.

"Not really. I don't want to be with them anymore. If I could fly, I don't know if I'd even tell them. I'd keep it a secret, and just be happy knowing what I could do."

"Why can't you fly?"

"I don't know. Maybe there's something wrong with me."

"I don't think there is."

"Thanks, Rudy."

"Maybe it's the rest of us that are wrong. And we're not supposed to be able to fly." Rudy smiled, hoping to make his sister feel better.

"No. Don't ever say that," she insisted. "We're not supposed to fall."

The next day, two before Christmas Eve, Donna and Rudy went to the flying games where all the reindeer went out to test their abilities.

Donna hated watching the games. But she loved Rudy and

wanted to see him win the games again. But unlike every set of games before, Rudy was scared.

"Why are you afraid?" she asked.

"Because it's so cold. I don't know if I'll be able to fly."

"Then don't do it, Rudy. Wait until the wind is not so cold or the snow is not so icy."

"I can't. If they see I can't fly when it's cold, then I'll never be any good to any-"

"To anyone? Are you afraid they'll treat you like they do me?"

"You don't understand."

"Maybe not. But I know what it's like to want to fly. You don't have to win the contests this year."

"I do."

"Okay. I'm going to tell them what happens when you get cold and afraid."

"Don't."

"But it's for your own good. It's important that you...I don't want anything to happen to you. You're all I..."

"If you tell them anything, I'll never speak to you again. And you'll be no friend of mine. You promised you wouldn't, Donna. You promised. Swear you won't tell them. Swear."

She didn't want to remain quiet. But she did.

Donna watched her brother go to the games. She watched him shiver and shake. And she watched him win contest after contest, until the very last one, a contest that required the reindeer to fly off the side of a cliff, fly straight up into the air, and return in a triumphant stance of glory.

He was afraid and cold and tired and she knew he didn't want to do it. But he had to prove that he was not like her. She didn't blame him for this, but it still hurt a little.

She watched him skip to the edge of the cliff, and she saw the fear in his eyes. He wasn't going to make it.

I'd like to tell you that the fear of seeing her brother fall off the cliff was all she needed to learn how to fly. But that's not what happened. Everyone was shocked to see Rudy fall off the side of the cliff. He'd always been their best flier. They were even more shocked to see Donna running towards the cliff edge, faster than any other reindeer could, and jumping after him. Of course, they knew she would not fly, but would fall as well.

It was a very long drop, so Donna and Rudy had a chance to speak as they plummeted to the icy rocks below.

"Rudy?" she cried as she fell. And there in front of her—more like falling below her—she saw him.

"Donna?"

"Don't be afraid," she cried. "Don't be afraid and fly. It's that simple."

"But I'm afraid."

"You're just cold. I'm not afraid, Rudy."

"But you could never fly. You're falling."

"I know. But it's Christmas. And I never have anything to give at this time. Until now. And my present for you is to make certain you fly. Think about Christmas. Think about what it means to you; and you will fly. Think about Mom and Dad and our home and your favorite things. Think about how much you love to fly. Think about how much you love the games."

And then, Rudy couldn't see Donna anymore. And he realized why.

He had stopped falling.

After Christmas Eve, the reindeer patrol searched the base of the cliff for days and days, until at last they found Donna's body, frozen almost to glass. Even Tabby seemed genuinely upset and sad. She called Donna a hero. Rudy cried and thanked Tabby, telling her and everyone else about how Donna had saved him. About how Donna had been his best friend and taught him to fly even when he was afraid. He would be braver because of her. And even if the other reindeer ever treated him badly in his future, he would be brave and kind and have hope. Just like Donna.

Even Santa said something kind about Donna, and Santa never bothered with the deer that couldn't fly. Not because he isn't one of the best people there ever was, but because the best of people are usually very busy and need to be shown grace themselves.

But Santa's words were lost on *Donna*. She couldn't hear them. She was too far away.

And the Donna she was now was not the Donna at the bottom of the cliff. Santa and Rudy and Tabby and all the other deer were all specks below her as her ghost soared through the winds and the clouds and the stars.

It was not cold. It was not dark. If anything, she felt very warm indeed. This, this is what she was meant for. And she didn't want to die any more. Not even on Christmas Eve, which she now liked. After all, it had now become a new sort of birthday.

# Mary Had a Little Lamb

We never hear the good news, only the bad. Usually about people we don't know. Sometimes about people we do. About cities or blocks just far enough away to not seem quite real but close enough for us each to say, "Thank god it wasn't me." Or, "Someday, someone's going to do something about this." And that's usually how it goes.

But sometimes the worst possible thing in the world actually happens to you. To you, instead of to someone else. Your life is destroyed and whatever hopes, plans or dreams you had are now a joke, and a sad one at that. And you fear nothing will ever change no matter how many new years there are to come. And with that fear comes a terrible dread. Not just for tomorrow. But for every tomorrow. And no matter how many tears you shed, no matter how soggy your pillow becomes, you still hope for a miracle you don't believe in.

But after a while, after there is some distance between you and that explosive thing, when life takes on a new direction, one you could never have expected, it seems like that original worst possible thing was actually the best thing ever. It's as if you had known what would come as a result, you yourself would be asking for that terrible thing to happen.

Or at least be grateful for it to happen sooner.

I was bitten by something a number of years ago. The bite changed me from what I was. And for that, I will always be thankful.

My mom's name was Mary. It's a popular name. I think she was named that because of a Catholic thing, but I can't remember. If I have any memory of her from when I was a boy, it was that she was both very sad and very afraid. And that fear manifested itself in a coddling, awful way of raising me. Consider me swaddled well into my adulthood.

She was obsessed with safety, as many mothers are, I suppose. But she was convinced that something terrible might one day happen to me. *Every* day. Her long, deep sighs at the end of every day were matched only by neurotic warnings the next day. My breakfast, which I'm happy to say she made for me every day, was pre-cut, just to give you an example. Thank God, I suppose, she didn't fancy herself a bird and present it to me half-digested. Thank God.

So I was taught to be careful of everything at all times, to be careful of *people*. To not offend them even if what they did was wrong, to never interrupt anyone, regardless of the circumstance. To move out of someone else's way no matter how far off they may be. And I was told to apologize for everything. She said that no one could be mad at someone who was saying, "I'm sorry."

My mother told me that my father was not a kind man, and he was prone to both drinking and violence, and not always in that order.

To be fair, a number of people in town said that this wasn't true, that he was a good man, but my mother said that you couldn't really know someone unless you lived with them. And people could always get worse. She considered it a great blessing the day he finally left home on a business trip and didn't come back. I remember that my mother laughed, almost hysterically, and said, "Now, at last, we are safe."

But that was not the case. At least, we never felt safe.

There was so much I didn't understand about the world I lived in. For the sake of safety, and for the peace of pleasing my mother, it felt acceptable that I had had the wool pulled over my eyes. For a while, at least. There was something inside me, though, that was growing, becoming. As if this idea of safety that had been lifted so high up, had somehow become cruel in its own way. I yearned to leave. And one day I did.

I moved to New York City in the early seventies. I see now that I knew the pursuit of safety above all else was a poor way to approach life, so I went someplace that was not safe.

New York was not as safe a place then as it is today. It was a time when gangs walked the streets and turf wars lasted for years.

My mother, of course, did not want me to work in New York. She had heard stories about New York City. Terrible stories. Still, I needed a job, and she considered financial security as a form of safety. And there really weren't many jobs in the small town I had been raised in.

I worked just off of 42nd street. I was an accountant, which was a very respectable job.

I worked with the same people every day. They were strangers to me. It was best to keep things professional, I reminded myself. Relationships aren't safe.

I walked to the Port Authority to catch my bus after work every day as well. And on the way there, I would pass through an area that would be considered 'up for bids' by the local gangs.

On some days, the Cat Brothers would take my money and give me a new bruise in exchange. On other days, it would be the Gorillas that tried to kill me. Other days it was someone else.

The strange part of it was, the area was nothing to desire. The streets were filled with garbage, the windows in the buildings were broken, the people in the tenements rarely ever ventured from their homes.

Everyone here was afraid. And maybe that's why I, too, belonged here.

It's interesting now when I think about the city during that time. There was so much potential. I could see it even then. Yet I lacked the power, even the courage to attempt anything. Even picking up a piece of trash off the street and putting it in the garbage would require an act of rebellion against my natural tendencies to leave things the way they were. I had been taught of course to see that trash carried germs and potential disease. Best to leave it there until someone trained in dealing with such potential dangers took to their job.

That was actually my approach to everything. Don't disturb and just go around the problem if possible. Though, for the area that was between my work and the Port Authority, there was no way around it.

It was Christmas Eve and I had decided, almost in stark contrast to how I was raised, to spend some time in Times Square.

Christmas in New York City, despite all the dangers, can be a very exciting thing. Christmas trees are everywhere. Salvation Army workers dressed like Santa are ringing bells on every corner. Steam rises like ghosts from the manholes.

Times Square is well known for its lights all year round, but during the holidays it can be overwhelming.

I wish I could tell you that I went home that Christmas Eve and had a quiet, and very safe, evening watching Christmas specials on television and counting my blessings.

After enjoying the lights, I decided it was time to go home. I didn't get far from Times Square when I was attacked and dragged into one of the back alleys of New York, in the area aptly named Hell's Kitchen.

At first, I thought it was one of the gangs that had finally tracked me down. Perhaps one of the Cat Brothers, or maybe I had accidentally wandered into Gorilla territory. But no, it wasn't even a human being that attacked me. It was a dog of some sort.

It bit into my arm and into my side. I don't remember how much blood I lost in those moments. But I remember crying and crying and crying. I remember screaming for help.

No one came.

No one ever came in those days in New York.

This dog that seemed more than a dog seemed to bite and chew and rip for hours, but that can't possibly be. I would surely have died after being savaged for that long.

And then the beast ran down the street, leaving me huddled and lying behind in the alley for the rest of Christmas Eve.

At the time, all I could think about was my father. I thought I was dying, and instead of thinking about my mother, I thought about him.

Was he really as bad as my mother said? Or was she perhaps scared of the life she had had with him? Was she scared because he would not let her remain the way she was? And what, if he saw me here, would he think of me now?

I'm not sure why I thought of that then. But I remember thinking that when I was attacked, I had good reason to be scared.

Being attacked almost brought something like a justification for the way I had lived. I always expected to be attacked, and was always scared. And I hated myself for that.

When I awoke in the alley the next day, I saw that my wounds had all but healed. I stood and looked around me. It all seemed different. I seemed different.

Had this given me a new overconfidence? I wasn't sure. It was like I'd become someone new, almost. I grabbed my briefcase and opened it to make certain I hadn't lost anything. I hadn't. But I really didn't care all that much if I had, and that was strange as well. I'd checked more out of habit than out of fear.

Something was different.

I stepped out of the alley into a cold, windy Christmas Day. New York, on Christmas Day, is practically empty.

A piece of paper that was caught in the wind brushed up against my leg. On any other day, I would have tried to kick it off, but not today. I picked up the loose paper, germs and all, and prepared to throw it in the garbage when I noticed what was written on it. It was a brochure for a Christmas Circus. In the brochure there was everything you would expect to find at a circus, but there was something more, something they called a man-beast, the world's only living werewolf.

I stuffed the paper in my pocket and proceeded home. When I got there, I called my mom and told her what had happened.

She ordered me home and told me that we would somehow

survive. That I didn't need to work in New York. Or anywhere that wasn't safe for that matter.

"No. It's okay. I'm fine," I replied.

I heard her begin to cry on the other side of the phone. I certainly didn't want that.

She demanded that I come home. And again I reminded her of my answer. I had realized something. I had been bitten by a beast, and instead of dying had found a new strength. I had gained something from that creature. And perhaps it had taken something from me.

I had been put in harm's way, and had come out feeling better than I ever had in my life. I had been a sheep, a lamb waiting for an unknown slaughterer. But now, I was beginning to feel like a wolf myself.

I have to explain this, though. Because I did not find myself wanting to be cruel, like the gangs that fought in the streets, or like the mental picture I had of my father that I tried to ignore.

No, I felt like a wolf because I felt I had the power to do the very things I always thought I should. The things that I wanted to do and thought were right but couldn't. I had a new strength to do what I was afraid to do before.

I would know when work resumed after the holidays. I would know when I returned to the office on 42$^{nd}$ street and walked in the company of strangers.

I returned to work on January third. It was a Monday. And as I entered the office, I found myself saying hello, very uncharacteristically, to my co-workers.

Surprisingly, they said hello in return.

I found that, when I asked, they actually began to speak to me about their lives. And sometimes even asked about me. And the more I learned about their stories, the more they learned about my own, although I told no one about the wolf that had bitten me.

Later, I overheard a few of them making jokes about 'being human' must have been my New Year's resolution. I guess I cannot be too upset with them. But it is ironic, isn't it? Considering what I had been bitten by, and what I felt like I was becoming.

On the way home from work, I did not lean in towards the buildings as I usually did on these walks. I walked in the middle of the sidewalk…at least, until I found myself surrounded by the Cat Brothers gang.

They pulled out their knives, or claws, as they called them. They asked for my money. And for the second time in the last few weeks, I said, "No".

I told them that they were only cats, and that my kind is never afraid of theirs.

They laughed. And then they stopped. And they began to cry, and to scream, and to wail.

For they discovered, to their horror, that they were not the only ones that had claws.

For some, like my mother, Christmas is about comfort. It's about feeling safe, secure, if only for one night a year.

But when I think of Christmas, I think about what it took to not be afraid for the other 364 days of the year. I think of what it took to become a new man. I remember the scraping, bleeding and shredding of the old.

And I am very, very grateful.

# THE LINK

A ll ghosts have chains. This, though, is not to scare people. It is actually quite the opposite. The chain is like an anchor; it holds the spirits on Earth, keeping them from floating away into eternity.

Every link of the chain was a link to the life that the ghost had lived.

For one particular businessman, now a ghost, these links were all he had that suggested that he had ever lived at all.

Every link of his chain reminded him of some cruelty or selfish moment of his existence (which he thought was not quite a fair criticism of him), because, as he remembered them, these were actually moments of shrewdness and good business.

It was a marvel how much of his life he could find along the links. But something was not right. This life he now carried with him was most burdensome. It had a certain weight to it. And he didn't want to carry it anymore; which was strange, especially for one who had been considered so wealthy by his still-mortal contemporaries.

And so he began to moan as all ghosts do. It was a shallow moan to be certain; not the kind of moan that suggests any real sense of pain. It was like a sigh of dull boredom, the kind of moan that suggests a distant frustration. Like an echo of a half-forgotten idea.

For your information, ghosts do not try to scare people. When it happens, it is a secondary, largely suburban occurrence. They are just moaning because of their lot. And that is all. Most of them simply do not understand why they are ghosts and unsettled, and their moans are deep, deep sighs of frustration.

What was also strange and unsettling about this businessman's chain was the fact that he could find no place at which it was actually attached to his ghostly body, yet he could not let go of it.

Furthermore, the chain trailed off to nothingness, becoming immaterial and quite invisible below him. It was almost as if it were bound to something he did not have the eyes to discern.

And again, it was heavy. Not so heavy that he couldn't float above the sky with the other ghosts. But so heavy that he always felt somehow forced to witness the terrible and sad lives of those that still lived below him.

He, like all ghosts, could rise only so far above the living; but then he'd always be drawn back to watch the homeless. Forced to gaze into prisons and watch the lonely and forgotten. He couldn't look away from the hungry or the poor, no matter how hard or how often he tried.

This is another reason why ghosts hate their chains. Not only do they suffer, but they are not allowed to wallow in just their own pain. They see it all around them.

"The poor were intolerable while I lived," the former businessman said. "Must I now spend all eternity looking at these lazy people, these burdens on the world? Curse this chain and curse them!"

The former businessman often tried to anticipate how the chain that bound him actually worked. But it did not act as chains should. There were no locks, no places for keys to undo their hold. The chain was almost alive, although such a word is not used in ghostly circles. It was like some sort of astral umbilical cord that could not be cut away from him.

What was also strange was that the more he tried to understand this chain, and the more he looked at it, the longer it seemed to grow, as if looking upon his life added to the weight of it.

Many of the other ghosts warned him that he was just making it worse. That once a ghost understands 'his' chain, it is unbearable for him and therefore them. The other ghosts told him that he should just accept that he would be struggling against the chain for all eternity in an attempt to forget the very things the chain linked him to.

So, for a good long time, he shut his eyes to the chain and the memories that were such an affliction upon his afterlife. And this made him moan all the louder.

After a while, the former businessman stopped talking to the other ghosts. They had nothing to say, really. Nothing that made this day different from the tomorrow to come or the yesterday that had gone.

The ghost still had hope, though. Surely, this had to be a terrible mistake. After all, he had no debt. He abhorred it. He owed no one. This must have been a clerical error in the book of life; perhaps one that would be corrected in time, when the ledger was found to be out of balance.

Of course, time is different for ghosts, and not to be counted upon in light of eternity.

And so, the afterlife went on. And on.

Daily, if such words of temporal measure are even applicable, he was drawn down to masses of the living, forced to hang as if he were a victim of the gallows among the sick, dying and starving.

From time to time, and only because it was a better alternative to watching the suffering, he would allow himself to remember what he'd been when he was alive. And when he did, he could only think of one person; his business partner.

He remembered almost nothing but his colleague. They had been so similar in their practices, in their collection of riches. Those who were not poor before dealing with them certainly were thereafter. The two men were inseparable, the same man really. At least, of course, before one of them died.

Yes, the name was Scrooge. That was his partner's name.
Ebenezer Scrooge.
And this man, this ghost and businessman, was Jacob Marley.

Something did not add up for Jacob Marley, and nothing bothers a former accountant more than something that does not add up.

Why was he here? Why was he a ghost forced to look upon the suffering? Why was he so bound by his former life?

And so, Marley began to watch Scrooge. Not the Scrooge of the past, of Marley's chain and memories, but Scrooge as he lived his current days. It had now been a number of years since Marley's death. And Scrooge still lived.

Even watching the living Scrooge proved difficult, for the chain did not allow Marley to look upon the old Ebenezer for long.

On a few occasions, Marley tried to wrap the chain around a lamppost or building in hopes of limiting the ghostly tides that pulled him through the city. These tides were like gusts of wind that drew the spiritual masses towards particularly sorrowful lives.

And sometimes, those strange gusts or rivers would surprisingly draw Marley back to Scrooge as if Scrooge, too, were a human being in misery.

This did not make any sense to Marley. Scrooge had his money. He also had Marley's money now as well. Scrooge had potentially everything and anything money could buy. Yet he bought nothing. Like Marley before him, he spent nothing, seeking warmth and sustenance from the accumulation of wealth rather than the comforts it might have made available to him.

Marley spent nearly an entire year thinking about this very notion; imagining what it would have meant for his own life to have used at least some of his wealth.

And then, one day, after thinking mostly about money, he noticed the people below him. He saw the living that really had no life at all. He saw the dying. He saw the hungry. He saw the lonely.

And his speculations upon what life might have been like had he spent his wealth upon himself, became something very different. How he wished he had given his money to *them*.

Why hadn't he spent what he had on *humanity?*

His accumulation of wealth could have filled their stomachs, could have bought them a place to eat, a place to sleep. His money could have bought them life.

There, in the cold, Marley began to wail and moan. But it was not like the unhappy groans of the other ghosts. No, these howls frightened even the other spirits.

This was not the sadness that comes as a result of not understanding one's place in the afterlife.

This was the pain of recognition.

This was the culmination of understanding.

He now understood his chain. The chain was invisible to him in life, and in death, only part of it was visible. That is the reason he could not see where it began or ended. He was linked to his fellow man, chained to the living, to the lives to which he might have made a difference.

He was not free of the poor and the suffering, but secured to them. As long as one of them was in prison, he was not free. As long as one was hungry, he could not truly be satisfied.

Marley was wrong about having no debt. This ghostly existence was a debtor's prison. And he certainly belonged here. He owed a debt to everyone in the world, to every person that came into his life. To every stomach he might have filled. To every sick child he might have used his riches to heal. To every debt he might have paid.

But how could he pay this debt now? Actually, he realized, how could anyone in any debtor's prison pay their debt once they were trapped there? How many, he wondered, did he himself send to debtor's prison? He dared not look at his chain for the answer.

No. It was too late.

Scrooge now had Marley's money.

Marley watched how cruel Scrooge was to Cratchett, Scrooge's small-minded clerk and assistant.

He noticed how sad Scrooge was, and was surprised at that. And the closer he looked, the more Scrooge's own chain (invisible to Scrooge, of course) came into focus for Marley.

Now there is something about Marley that bears mentioning at this moment. Marley abhorred debt. He had always been very good at saving things. And so Marley chose to try to save his old friend, Ebenezer Scrooge, from suffering the same fate he had.

Marley's own escape from these nether regions was immaterial now. As so many things are in the world of spirits and the afterlife.

But how could he save anyone else in his current state? He certainly did not have any freedom of movement. All he had was his chain.

But he was a ghost. Maybe he could haunt Scrooge. Maybe he could scare Scrooge into changing.

He tried to speak to the other ghosts, but they knew nothing of even the type of thing he was considering.

"Scare to save?" they moaned. "We warned you that you would go mad!"

But after meeting with one hopeless ghost after another he finally chanced upon the discovery that there were special Ghosts of Christmas that might be inclined to help him.

Christmas had always been a nuisance to Marley, a Aday defined more by losses in the ledger than by gain.

But Christmas was also a day, at least in spirit, when the needs of one's fellow man were most naturally considered.

So, Marley thought about the possibility of using this particular day to free Scrooge from his own growing chain, if such a thing were possible. Scrooge needed to see his chain, and Marley hoped the Ghosts of Christmas would help him.

There were many Ghosts of Christmas. Most had been people that died on Christmas Day over the many years of history. And some had simply been people who so loved Christmas that they were drawn to be such creatures in the afterlife. They haunted with love, and moved men to acts of extraordinary kindness and secret giving. They were also very amused to find Marley chaining himself to a Christmas tree in the slum district of the city. He told them later that he did this to try to gain their attention.

And so they encircled Marley, and there were many of them,

hoping to understand what this strange, petty ghost so wanted. Did he desire to be like them? Is that why he lashed himself to the tree?

"There is a man," cried Marley, "who is so much like me, and is living the same life I did. Saving him would be like saving myself. He was my business partner in life. I would not like to see him in death."

The Ghosts of Christmas listened to this man who could only be a ghost like this with a chain of such length due to great selfishness, and his begging moved them.

"I am not certain what it was that allowed me to see what I have lost, but I would like you to give Ebenezer a taste of his chain. His will be longer than even mine if he lives much longer. I'm sorry for the life I lived. If I had only seen my chain before. Can you let Scrooge see his own? Can you let him know what will happen if he continues living this way, continues adding link after link? Let him see what will happen if he ignores the debt he owes those in need?"

The Ghosts of Christmas told Marley that there would be a terrible price to be paid for doing such a thing. Marley would therefore be called upon to pay this cost. Marley understood debt. He understood that charity required someone to be charitable. So he agreed to the Christmas Ghosts' demands, although the price he would pay was almost too terrible to even think about.

The Ghosts discussed it amongst themselves and it was decided that three of them would visit this Ebenezer Scrooge. They would show him certain links in Scrooge's own chain. Scrooge would see the past, see all he had lost in his attempts to gain. He would be shown the needs of his fellow man in the present, both known and unknown. And Scrooge would see his last days, and the final forging of the chain that would hold him for all eternity, and held him even now while he still lived.

And so one Christmas Eve, seven years after the death of Jacob Marley, Ebenezer Scrooge was confronted by the super-natural. And in that single night, Scrooge re-lived his own lifetime. That sleepless eve, Ebenezer's eyes were opened to all that he had failed to see. And miraculously, Scrooge was freed of his chain and learned to keep Christmas in his heart. For all the days to come.

It was just as Marley had hoped.

Scrooge called it a Christmas miracle.

And the wealth that had been Marley's and Scrooge's became a lifeline in the city.

Marley himself returned to the mass of spirits to be pulled through the city. Scrooge had been saved. Marley had not.

Some of the other ghosts looked at him and looked away almost immediately. They were terrified by what they saw.

It was no longer only Marley's chain that Marley carried, but Scrooge's as well.

Scrooge would claim he saw the truth, but that wasn't enough. Someone had to take his chain. That was the cost the Christmas spirits demanded. And so Scrooge's chain was added to Marley's. Marley's chain more than doubled.

*How evil he must have been,* some of the other ghosts thought, as they came to understand their own chains. *How evil he must be.*

Yet, despite how long the chain now was for the ghost of Jacob Marley, it was not as heavy as it had been before.

And in time, Jacob learned that he could float a little higher above the city, a little further with this chain…although not far enough to escape the city or the needs of his fellow man.

And in his heart, Jacob Marley no longer wished to.

# Poison Cookies

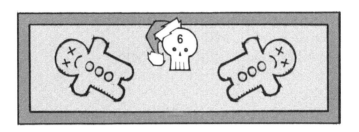

I don't belong here. It's a conspiracy and it isn't fair. I should never have been left for so long. It was just an attempted crime, really. They say I'm a patient in this hospital, but that's not true, I'm a prisoner.

He's keeping me here. I know he is. All the doctors and the nurses are his little helpers. They're on his good list. And they're keeping me trapped because of what I tried to do to him when I was seven years old. They're keeping me here so that they get their presents and gifts on Christmas morning.

He's still angry about that one year. Well, fat man, I can remember, too. I remember the Christmas I tried to kill you, Santa Claus. You give presents to everyone else in the world. But I will never forget what you took from me.

He's a scary guy. You have to admit that. And it's got nothing to do with the fact that he can live in the coldest place on Earth or considers elves his contemporaries. He's a scary guy because he's always watching you. If you're bad or good, while you're awake or when you sleep, if you're shouting or pouting, he knows.

And people here say I'm sick.

Think about it. Not only is he watching us, he's judging us. Some are good enough for the nice list. Some aren't. And those that aren't are on the naughty list. They're not good enough for his gifts.

But it's worse than that. It really is.

Because it's not just about behavior, and I've spent a lot of time thinking about this. Don't try to interrupt me. I've had thirty-five years to think this through. Have you?

When I was five years old, and living with my parents in our home in Chicago, I, like every other kid in the world, wanted everything. I wanted a teddy bear, a metal steam shovel, a boomerang, a frisbee, a yo-yo, a jack-in-the-box, a train, an erector set, some stuffed animals, boxing balloons and plastic dinosaurs.

I got everything I wanted except the boomerang.

Now, I'm not greedy. I'm not. No. Don't think that. I had my list of what I wanted. Santa's got his lists too. No one says he's greedy.

But with all those presents he was also giving me a message. And that was that he was not pleased with my performance.

My parents tried to help me with my pain and disappointment. They told me that Santa probably didn't bring me the boomerang because he thought I was too young to have it. That maybe Santa would bring me one in a year or two.

But I knew the truth.

I hadn't done so well in English the year before, and Santa was watching. My grades didn't pass his tests.

So I studied and studied and worked and worked and worked. I did everything I possibly could to be the best kid in the world.

And I was. Even my parents talked about what a good kid I was. In fact, it was a bad year for them and they said I made it better. My Dad lost his job and we had to leave our house and move north to an apartment in Sheboygan, Wisconsin of all places. My parents told me not to hope for too much from Santa that Christmas, but I knew that they didn't understand. I was perfect. My grades were great. I was as good as good can be. I was good even for goodness' sake.

And you know what I got for Christmas that year? You know what I got? A book, some socks, and a few Lincoln Logs that actually look like they had been played with by the elves. Can you believe it? If my parents had actually bought my presents that year, as bad as it was, they could probably have afforded more. And Santa, who's got an entire toy factory, did that to me after I'd been perfect. Well, maybe not perfect, but as perfect as a kid could be.

The truth was that Santa didn't care what you did or didn't do. He didn't care if you were bad or good. I had friends at school that got bad grades, pulled their sister's hair, beat on losers after class and were basically rotten kids. And they got loads of toys from Santa.

And you know why? It's because their parents were rich.

Santa's all about the money.

I realized then what a cruel, fat monster Santa was. Naughty and Nice was not as black and white as the fat man that dressed in red made us all think it was.

And I saw it. I saw him for what he was.

He had to die. He did. He had to pay for being so unfair.

They say that if you don't believe in Santa, it's like automatically being put on the "Naughty" list. He simply will not come to your house, and that means your parents get stuck buying you toys.

So when I decided to kill him the next year, I pretended to believe in him like I always had in the past. Even when the other kids at the school were saying he wasn't real. Even when they laughed at me for saying he was.

He was always watching. I had to be smart about this. I couldn't let him—or anyone else for that matter—see what I was planning.

But how to kill him? That was the question. What was his weakness?

The answer was obvious. Just look at the belly. His want for milk and cookies would be his undoing. Serves him right. He eats and drinks milk and cookies from every kid in the entire world. What a pig. He was an addict.

I checked with my friends. The cookies were always eaten. Sometimes the milk wasn't drunk, though.

45

So, poison cookies were the answer.

He'd eat them even if he didn't want to. He had no choice… he was a cookie junkie. And celebrating the twelve days of Christmas is not the same as being part of a twelve-step program. Santa was sick. I was going to make him sicker.

We were now living back in Chicago, by the way. My father had changed jobs and my parents had promised that Santa would be bringing more that year because of my good behavior. But it had nothing to do with how good I was. My parents now had more money. It was as simple as that.

So I asked my Mom if that year, that Christmas, I could make the cookie batter all by myself.

She smiled and said, "Sure". Of course, I had to agree to her pulling out the ingredients to the Double-Double Chocolate Chip cookies, the favorite cookie of Santa and fathers alike. But when she wasn't looking, I added rat poison to the mix.

'Not a creature was stirring, not even a mouse', indeed.

And that's how I tried to kill Santa Claus.

You know what I found the next morning? Every present I had asked for including a boomerang.

You know what else I found?

My parents were dead under the tree. He took them from me. He took my family.

I made them promise not to eat the cookies the night before. They promised. They knew they were for Santa and Santa only. And Santa tricked them, and then he gave me everything I wanted, if only to spite me.

I called the police immediately. I told them my story. I told them what Santa had done. I told them I was a witness to murder.

My story hasn't changed in all these thirty-five years. It never will.

The one thing I do know is that my parents didn't eat the cookies, no matter what anyone says. They couldn't have. They promised not to.

And they would never lie to me.

# THE HAUNTING DOLL

This is the story of a Christmas present. One that haunts still to this day.

My mother, who has long given up her German name of Hilma, was born in 1939, the beginning of World War II, in Nazi-occupied Poland. My mom's first home was not a home, but a series of homes. They were spread out and hidden throughout Nazi-occupied Poland. The dangers brought by German troop movements and by invading Russian soldiers forced my mom's family to move from one area to another, hiding, almost playing cat and mouse. It wasn't that they were considered dangerous or enemies of the Reich. It was more that whenever danger came close, they moved to where the danger wasn't; and this became more and more difficult as the war advanced through Europe.

The one constant in my mom's life was her doll. It was a Christmas gift.

Now the doll itself was nothing compared to the dolls of today. It didn't cry, it didn't hold its burp, and it didn't wet its pants. And perhaps, when you put it that way, my mom's doll was far superior to dolls today because it didn't require any work, or batteries, to love it.

The doll itself was not all that beautiful either. It wasn't porcelain, and it didn't wear lace. Its body was made of wood; a hunk of wood, actually, that was roughly carved into the shape of a body. Over this crude wooden figure was a dress, not particularly beautiful, and probably sewn from a scrap of cloth that hadn't been able to be used to patch a real dress. The head was a much better-sculpted piece of wood. There was no hair—only the shape of hair—because it, too, was part of the carved form. And finally, there was some paint on the head to make the doll's carved hair look brown and her eyes look blue and her lips look red and her skin look, well, how skin looks.

But regardless of what you're imagining, the doll was loved in that way only small girls are able to love a doll. And it was my mom's love for that doll that made it beautiful.

Finding a new place to live at the end of World War II was difficult. This was a time when almost all of Europe was being rebuilt after the terrible destruction that had turned so much of the continent into little more than rubble. Most buildings have at least four walls. In Germany, after the war and destruction, the buildings that were left had maybe one wall or two, as if the homes themselves now stood like giant doll houses. But even then, these houses were still not fit to live in, and not just because of the snow or rain or cold. Many would collapse just by walking through them.

So most people, including my mom's family, were housed in refugee camps before being moved out into the country and into other people's homes. As a result, many families were divided and spread throughout the country.

My mom's family would never be in the same place together again, and some were even trapped in Russian-occupied East Germany.

My mom, her doll, her mother, and two of her brothers ended up living in a small country house with another family. The house was in Wemlighausen, Germany.

And that family had a daughter.

Her name was Gudrun but there was very little 'good' about her. Sometimes children are called little monsters. And that is usually an unfair thing to say. But in the case of Gudrun, it was very true.

Maybe that IS being unfair. My mom, who was there and who told me this story, is probably reading these words and thinking that I'm being unfair. After all, Gudrun was just a little girl, and my mom was moving away. What made Gudrun not-so-good was the fact that she coveted my mom's doll: the one by which all other dolls might be measured and judged inferior.

Gudrun was four years old and my mom was now ten.

It's important to point out that Gudrun had many dolls of her own; she just didn't have the one that belonged to my mom.

The housing was temporary and the quarters were cramped. My mom and her family were all crammed into two small rooms, waiting for word to come that Germany was livable again, or that some other option had presented itself.

'Grossmutter' or Grandmother, my mom's mom's mom, sent word that there was room for them in Milwaukee, Wisconsin. And that they should come and live with her.

And when my mom's family prepared to leave for America, Gudrun pitched a fit. Not because my mom was leaving, but because the doll was.

This was the tantrum to end all tantrums; the kind of foot-stomping, breath-holding, red-faced tantrum that makes people afraid to have children.

And it didn't subside. This child was a brat, incapable of even seeing the harm she was causing.

My mom's mom had a name that was almost impossible to pronounce. I knew her as Oma, but her real name was Euphresina. Yes, Euphresina. She had learned that life was filled with loss. She was widowed twice; trampled by a bull; had had her leg ripped open by a stage coach, a wound that never fully healed; and now, half of her family—including some of her daughters—were trapped in East Germany, and would not be part of the trip to America.

All this loss changes a person. Whether for good or bad, Euphresina, my Oma, learned not to hold onto anything too tightly because it could be taken away so easily. She learned how to live and laugh with nothing, though this time was not really a time of laughter.

And with Gudrun, it was a time of bellowing.

And so, just before leaving Germany for America, with no real possessions of her own, Euphresina made my mom give up her one love. To be fair to Oma, it was a way to thank the family that had taken them all in. But that's being fair to Oma, not necessarily to my mom.

My mom was forced to give her doll to Gudrun. Forced to appease the abysmal behavior of a greedy child. And it broke her heart.

This, of course, made the train trip across Europe, and then the ocean liner voyage across the Atlantic to America, a lot more difficult. And lonely for my mother. But she did get to experience seeing the Statue of Liberty from a boat coming into New York City Harbor.

I wonder sometimes, when my mom saw Lady Liberty, holding a torch in one hand, and a tablet in the other, if she wasn't thinking a little about what she wasn't holding, and what that undeserving child in Germany was.

My mom and her family settled in Milwaukee, Wisconsin to live with her Grandmother. There were—and still are—many breweries there, and therefore was a beloved place for many Germans, though I am not certain that that was the reason Grossmutter settled there.

And though there were people who came into my mom's life who would buy her dolls—much better ones actually—it was not the same. They were never the same.

But there are some losses, some wounds, like those my Oma dealt with, that never fully heal.

And maybe, just maybe, they aren't supposed to.

You see, as my mom describes it, the pain of loss is also something not worth holding onto.

And so, growing up, every time I would be bullied by someone who wanted something I had, my mom was there to remind me that if people wanted it so badly, to just let them have it. Or if I was in an argument and the outcome really didn't matter, my mom was there to tell me that I should just give in and let the other person have their dignity. Or, if something I had was stolen, to not hold onto the anger too long. And to remember that in this life, things would always be taken from me. That's life.

But she also wanted me to know that what is taken from me is not me. No one can take anything of me, just from me. I am not diminished. Not one bit. And sometimes, for me to grow, I was lucky when indeed I had to go with less than I had had before.

I don't believe this, though, because I was stone and my mom was water—that her constant dripping somehow wore a hole in my stone resolve. No. I believe what my mom says to be true because I have seen it.

Fifty years after my mom left Germany, she returned to visit some of her sisters and other family members. She had returned a number of times before then, but this was the fiftieth anniversary of her original departure, so she went again. It was upon this visit that one of her sisters told her that Gudrun wanted to see her.

My mom never forgot Gudrun; and now, neither will I.

My mother met Gudrun one morning in Germany over coffee and cake.

And while they sat, now two grown women entering their golden years, Gudrun began to tell my mother about how she had become a mother herself. She told my mom about her children. And then about how she became a grandmother a number of times over.

The two women shared pictures and exchanged their stories of new families and change and then finally, when the cake was gone, and the coffee was getting cold, Gudrun began to talk about the doll.

Gudrun told my mom about how she had told her children the story of her childhood envy and how she had taken the one thing a little girl had in the world. Gudrun told her children and her children's children the story many times. And taught them a very different lesson than the one my mom taught me, but one no less important, no less valuable.

Gudrun taught her children and grandchildren that it is a terrible thing to ever want what someone else has. To ever covet and take at the expense of someone else. Because to want from someone else so badly, is to diminish oneself. And there are some things, once taken, you can't give back.

Gudrun begged my mom's forgiveness right there and told her that this was the most valuable lesson she could give her children.

My mom, being who she was, pretended that she hadn't given it another thought.

Gudrun wished that she still had the doll to return to my mom.

My mom told her that she was just grateful that they, as mothers, could teach their children both such important lessons. And how grateful she was that such good things could come from such a little doll.

Gudrun pulled out a handkerchief from her purse. She again told my mom that she wished she still had the doll. She began to unfold the handkerchief. And then showed my mom what she had brought for her.

Gudrun still had the head. She still had the doll's head.

The body had long ago splintered and broken apart. And the clothing it had worn—barely able to be called clothing in the first place—had torn and fallen to pieces. But the head remained, paint all but worn away…a well-loved doll indeed.

Gudrun passed the head of the doll to my mom, returning what she had taken so long ago.

So there was good in Gudrun after all. And now there was good in her children and children's children too. All because my mom had lost the one thing she had.

My mom, overwhelmed, returned to America and put the doll's head in her glass cabinet. This is the place where her most valuable pieces of China and silver and crystal are kept. And the doll's head is there still, to this day.

My mom is of a certain age right now where she wants me to wander the house and let her know the things she has that she should leave me when she dies. It's a terrible question, and one that I really don't answer because I don't want to think like that, and I don't want to even prepare for that kind of loss.

That said, I have claimed the doll head, a Christmas present that haunts still.

My mom laughs and calls me a strange boy, not seeing that that head is a story, the story of all of us, and in some ways, the secret of how to live life.

I wonder sometimes if my mom would still have the doll today if it had not been taken from her before her voyage to America. Would it have just been a doll that sat in a corner and was forgotten and thrown out? I wonder if the doll was more cherished out of Gudrun's guilt than of my mom's love for it? Did Gudrun, like the Ancient Mariner, carry it and protect it out of shame? And I wonder if having the doll taken away in the first place didn't somehow make my mom love it more. And people more. You see, to my knowledge, my mom has never lost a friendship. She's now been married to my dad for more than fifty years. And is beloved for her character and kindness by all who call her friend. She knows how to keep things, having learned from having lost them.

Maybe losing teaches us how to love and what to love.

Maybe losing teaches us the worth of what we have and what we've had.

I like to think so. I like to live as if it were so, if only in anticipation of being ready to receive back the things I've lost in a way that defies expectation.

Perhaps this isn't the type of story you expected to find in a book of this sort. But it certainly has a lot to do with spirits, some better than others. And, after all, there was a beheading.

# THE FRANKINCENSE MONSTER

It was going to be a monster.

That's what the weatherman said. It was going to be a White Christmas unlike any that New Yorkers could remember.

The snow that was forecast wasn't in inches…it was in feet.

And for those that made their home on the island of Manhattan, the fear of how long this blizzard of blizzards would last was a cold thought indeed.

First, you should know that snow shovels are useless in New York City. They're almost a novelty. In fact, owning one is the first sign of someone who just moved in from the suburbs. This is because it rarely snows. And when it really does snow, the last thing you even want your neighbor to have is a shovel. And that's the last thing he wants you to have.

The problem is that there's never enough space in New York when it's summer and it's sunny out. But when it snows, the city that never sleeps goes into hibernation. And that's because if you even had a shovel full of snow, there'd be no place to throw it. There are no front-yards or backyards or side-yards in the city. No ditches to throw the snow from the streets into. No place to toss the fluffy white stuff without hitting a 'neighbor' in the face.

And of all the things that can 'make it' in New York, fluffy isn't one of them.

There was no telling how long a pile of snow on your doorstep would last.

So everyone was dreading the storm. Most New Yorkers

joke that you can always tell the tourists because they are the ones walking around looking up at the skyscrapers. But on this, the afternoon of December 24th, everyone was looking up. Because a cloud as big as the island had come to rest above their heads.

And no one was happy about this, least of all the manager of the Grace Children's Christmas Day benefit.

Every year on Christmas Day, a gathering took place at the foot of New York's largest tree in Central Park. Every year, the children of the city (those who did not have a big family get-together or came from families that could not afford presents) would venture out on Christmas morning from their homes. They came to visit the giant tree and celebrate Christmas and the spirit of love and sharing that comes over the entire world that most special of special days.

Every December 24th for the last fourteen or fifteen years, presents would be delivered late in the evening to this place, for the children to find the next day.

The gifts, in the true spirit of Christmas, would be sent anonymously, without being signed. Gifts given without the need for a thank-you card. Gifts given because it was Christmas.

But with the announcement of the impending storm and the fact that over a foot of snow had already buried Connecticut and Jersey, the airports closed down and the shipment of toys was postponed until December 26th.

Businesses were closing early. People were leaving the city by cars, buses, and trains; and even in the middle of winter, some were making their exit on bicycles and on roller blades.

And then it began to snow.

But the weatherman was wrong about the inches and the feet.

There was but one flake that fell from that giant cloud.

There was only one tiny flake that danced on the winds above the city, and looked for a spot to call home. One flake that made for the giant tree in the heart of Central Park.

It looped and ducked and fell as if it were showing off what it could do.

It fell past the decorations and even slowed here and there as if it were enjoying its own reflections in the bulbs and lights that hung there.

It fell. And fell and fell. And just when it seemed like it would finally come to rest at the foot of the tree, the lone flake was lifted by the wind again, and flew off to another part of the city.

It wasn't a miracle. At least it wouldn't be considered one then. It stood maybe ten feet tall, this creature. This mass that moved through the back alleys of the area that was once called Hell's Kitchen, New York.

Most people in the city did not believe their eyes when they saw it, and that's why news of the creature did not spread. In New York, you see a lot of strange things and you learn pretty quickly not to pay too much attention to any of it. And you learn not to look too long down the darker streets or the thin alleys that separate one building from another.

But if anyone had really bothered to look at the creature, they would have realized that this was not a human being at all. It wasn't a living creature either. It was more mechanical. But not in the way you would expect a machine or a robot to operate.

This was a creature made up completely of toys.

Apart from the sheer size and shape of its body, its face was the most notable of its features. It had a teddy bear for a nose. Its mouth was a metal steam shovel. It had boomerang ears. One eye was a frisbee. The other eye was the looped string of a yo-yo. The yo-yo itself circled up and down like a monocle.

The back of the creature was almost hunched. Around this hunch, which was actually a jack-in-the-box, there was a toy train that encircled the box, sounding its horn from time to time and even puffing out a small cloud of steam every once in a while.

Its fingers were built from an old erector set. The creature's legs were made of a wide assortment of stuffed animals, boxing balloons and plastic dinosaurs. It was a sight to behold.

The first person to even approach the creature was a little boy named William.

William smiled at the creature.

"I've never seen a toy store that could walk before," said William, having already developed a great suspicion of things and knowing everything had a price.

"Why do you think I'm a toy store?"

"Because you have so many toys on you."

"I'm not a toy store. Maybe I'm just a friend."

"Well, I'm not supposed to talk to strangers, and I'm sure you would count as one."

With that, William ran up the block, almost forgetting right away about the creature he had spoken to.

And so the creature lumbered on down the streets, not quite sure what he was or how he came to be. He remembered the junkyard. He remembered the wind lifting him off the ground and he remembered movement for the first time. He remembered a single speck of snow and a giant cloud. But that was all.

The next person that came upon him was a little girl named Janna.

She looked at him.

He looked down at her.

He tried to make his steam-shovel mouth smile, but it was difficult. The metal didn't bend. Not even a little. Janna began to cry and then she began to scream and then she too ran away from the creature.

The creature itself was now confused. The first boy didn't recognize it as a friend. And it had just scared the girl. Didn't they see what it was? It wasn't just a toy. It was every toy. Every toy given the opportunity to play back with the child that wanted to play with it. Why couldn't anyone see this?

Another girl, who was just a little older than ten, walked away from its pleadings to play, telling it that she was too old to play with toys.

And still another boy, one that seemed to understand at last what it was, attempted to put his arms around the creature,

57

but found that even the creature's leg was too big to get his arms around.

"I think that when I get bigger I'll be able to play with you. You're too big for me," said the boy.

"And when you get bigger, you'll be older; will you still want to play?" The creature moved on with a new and sad sense of understanding.

The boy walked away sadly, wanting to play but not knowing how. There was too much of the creature to have, to understand, to hold onto or to be friends with. It was too big to be loved. And that was the problem.

The creature wandered all Christmas Eve night, wondering why it was here, hoping for some sort of reason to satisfy the etch-a-sketch that was scratching out possibilities and erasing them at a feverish pace.

And then it came upon the tree, the tree in Central Park. It was the tree that didn't have any presents, the children's party tree.

The creature was surprised by what it saw. Hundreds of chairs were in place, but they were empty and waiting to be filled. He saw posters for the Grace Children's Christmas Day benefit.

But what captured its interest the most was not what was there, but was not. There was nothing under the tree. And the creature knew that this was not right.

It looked at the tree, which, from where it stood, seemed less like a tree and more like a giant green arrow pointing up to the sky.

It stared and questioned and wondered.

Where were the presents?

It didn't understand.

And then it turned, and saw the chairs set up behind it. It saw the sign for the children's benefit. It saw that there were no gifts for the children. It pieced together what was happening.

And then it saw signs that said things like 'Peace on Earth' on them. 'Peace'? There's that word again. No, not exactly.

'*Piece*' is the word it had been thinking about.

The monster took off one of its boomerang ears and laid it under the tree. But that did not seem to be enough. There were many chairs. There would be many children.

It read words that said 'Christmas was a Gift to all Mankind.' It wondered again. "*…Gift For All…*"

It looked at the empty chairs. And it thought about the children.

The creature felt something growing inside of it. It was an understanding of a gift that was not just meant to be given, but also meant to be broken; an idea that was bigger than Christmas or any single holiday, a thought so big the creature felt like it was going to explode.

And its metal, steam-shovel mouth almost seemed to smile.

But that's impossible.

The snow never fell. And the presents never arrived. The next morning, all the children came and all the adults feared a lot of unhappy children. But everyone was surprised to find yo-yos and trains and dolls and teddy bears and toys and punching balloons and plastic dinosaurs and erector sets everywhere. There was more than enough for every child there.

There was more than enough.

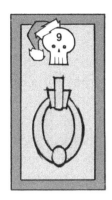

# You Better
# Watch Out

For some, this is not, and I repeat, not a merry time of year. There are no glad tidings and no comforts to speak of. And there is very little joy.

The holidays can bring reminders of parents who are gone, or friendships that were lost, or even of potentials that up 'til now have gone unrealized.

And this can be a good and healthy thing, to consider one's losses along with the gains. To think about what we have lost is to remember what we were first given. And so, if you are sad this time of year, don't feel too badly, because it could be worse. You could feel nothing at all.

You could be like the population in the city of Grey Falls.

If you've never heard of Grey Falls, Montana, it's because it no longer exists in any real sense of the word. It's a ghost town filled with broken buildings and skeletons and strange mysteries. If you have indeed heard of Grey Falls, then you must be a paranormal investigator, or ghost hunter, or even a psychic of sorts, because those are the only types of people that are drawn to visit the remains of Grey Falls now.

Some of these paranormal investigators have suggested that there are strange metaphysical tremors to be recorded on certain types of machines, which suggest that those who once made their homes in Grey Falls live there still. They claim to almost hear a knocking. Some fiction writers have suggested that it is as if the people in this town were somehow trapped and unable to get out. That they are constantly pounding on the walls of some unseen prison, begging to be free. But that's not the true story. It's quite the opposite, actually.

In the 1920's, Grey Falls was, on the surface, a beautiful and picturesque little city peopled with everything from a mayor to a barber to a town sheriff to teachers and more.

Being located in the heart of Montana, snow was pretty common. In fact, people didn't just expect a white Christmas; they could bank on white Thanksgivings, white President Days and even white Easters, which you would think would make hunting for brightly-colored Easter eggs a whole lot easier.

But there was something wrong with the people of Grey Falls, something cold and unforgiving. You see, it wasn't a white Christmas they expected; it was a white December 25th. And as far as Thanksgivings go, they were just two days at the end of November. Gratitude was not a part of their calendar. February was just cold. Spring held no new promises for them. Even birthdays went unremembered. And it wasn't due to religious affiliations, either. The people just did not care.

There really wasn't a tragedy or a loss to point to, at least not one any one bothered to recall, but people just sort of stopped celebrating or fussing for much of anything. There were no more decorations, no more attempts to make much of anything special, let alone Christmas.

There was no charity—not in their actions and not in their hearts.

And so it was that one day, a stranger came into town, just before war broke out in Europe. He'd been walking for a long time and needed a place to stay. He carried an old briefcase and had a long coat. He walked from door to door and knocked on each one, asking if he could stay the night.

He was a salesman, selling white correction ribbon for typewriters. In case you're not familiar with what this is, let me explain.

Say you took a white piece of paper, put it in a typewriter and typed a story with it. And then let's say you put this white correction ribbon in and retyped the whole story, with every letter of every word being retyped in the very same place on the paper. If you looked at the sheet after this was over, you'd be

left with only a white sheet of paper. There'd be nothing there…
nothing except very faint impressions that suggested a story had
been written. But really, it would be as if nothing had been typed
there at all. That's what this salesman sold, correction ribbon.
It was something especially helpful for covering up mistakes.
Think of it as an early form of correction fluid or white out. Or a
delete button that has to be pressed over and over again.

The salesman was cold, and he was thin, and even if he had
been offered some food, he couldn't possibly have eaten that
much. Nevertheless, everyone in the town ignored him. Everyone
shut his or her door to him. He begged in the name of Christmas.
And even those you'd expect to be inclined to help someone in
need, ignored him.

The salesman would come to the door, ask for something to
eat and a place to rest his feet for the night. He'd even offer some
correction ribbon in exchange for their charity Every time he was
told "No", he'd cough a little and then move on.

And then he was gone.

About a week later, the townspeople themselves began to
cough.

They coughed a deep irritating cough that no one could quite
understand. Were they coughing from their throats, or from their
heads, or from their lungs, or where?

What was most distressing about this cough, was that it
continued. It never went away. And it hurt.

After a while, the people even stopped going to the doctor,
accepting this as part of their life now. The doctor himself had
stopped prescribing anything for the cough, and in fact wouldn't
even answer the door if he heard someone cough on the other side.

When winter gave way to spring, the townsfolk continued to
cough.

Often times, their conversations were so interspersed with
coughing fits that they just stopped talking to each other outright.

Summer bowed to autumn and soon it began snowing again.
It snowed off and on until Christmas Eve, when another big
snow storm hit.

Most people stayed at home and the streets were—not

surprisingly—empty. Which made it, of course, very surprising when there was a knocking at every door in town.

The salesman had returned. This time he was offering cough syrup.

Again he asked for shelter—for a place to rest and a moment of respite from the storm.

The town librarian, who prided herself on remembering every cover of every book in her care, even remembered him from the year before.

But just like before, he was turned away. Turned away by everyone.

Door after door was shut in his face. And so he walked out of town. And the snow continued to fall. It continued all through Christmas and into the next year.

The snow got so heavy after a while that the phone lines began to snap and fall and the people could no longer call each other.

It piled up so high that the roofs of the poorest houses began to fall in under the weight of the snow. But they were only the first. Eventually, there were no houses that were safe. Even official buildings belonging to the most important people in town were collapsing from heaviness of snow.

And through it all there was the sound of knocking, a rapping at the door for shelter, for kindness, for pity.

But no one answered.

No one knew how much snow was falling or how much had fallen. Six feet at least. Yes, by the time they breathed their last and gave into numbness and the cold, they were six feet under.

If you were to look at the town from the sky, you would see no town at all.

It was as if the town was like a giant mistake that had just been whited out.

Some have said the knocking heard today is from those who had once tried to get out of Grey Falls, those who had been trapped there. But that's not the true story.

It's quite the opposite, actually.

# THE PEOPLE UNDER THE STARS

Once, long ago, years before the age of enlightenment and the industrial revolution, this was a world of shadow and mystery.

It was a time when some men, in their want for power and knowledge, lived in great haste in their pursuits and were transformed into monsters. These transformations were generally the result of risks taken in early scientific experimentation and arcane ritual. And those monsters lived amongst us. And preyed upon us.

People disappeared all the time in those dark ages and were consumed by these very creatures.

It was to be expected.

But some of these proto-scientists did not make the same mistakes as the others. They grew in knowledge and wisdom slowly. They advanced in technology and logic without foolishly experimenting upon themselves. Instead, they learned from nature and the common earth and by the careful study of cause and effect.

They learned how to fight the monsters.

So men were armed with bags full of stakes and crosses and the knowledge of what to do if they ever faced a vampire.

Everyone now carried matches because they knew the Frankenstein Monster hated fire.

Werewolves feared silver, and so every policeman had at least one silver bullet on him at all times.

The creatures had not expected anyone to gain such

knowledge and not become like them. These humans knew of the monsters' weaknesses, and had become so bold that the monsters became afraid for their very survival.

So the beasts that had been men retreated even further into the shadows, becoming the stuff of fairy tales and children's stories.

And soon, there were no more shadows at all...except of course, for those cast by people themselves.

But what happened to the monsters? Where did they go?

Much has been said about the Bermuda Triangle and the many terrible things that have happened there. And most of it is true. And the reason for these terrible and tragic losses is that there is an island in the Bermuda Triangle upon which all the monsters and myths of the past now dwell.

In the world of man, they learned fear. But here, there is nothing for them to be afraid of...except for one night of the year. On Christmas Eve, they all burrow into the earth and cover themselves from the night itself.

For on that night, a star shines on the island. It shines bright and bold and carries with it a terrible curse—those that are caught within the star's rays are transformed into the very people they would have become if they had never become monsters at all.

This is the story of a gargoyle who had grown tired of being a monster.

"I am weary. To sit and wait for nothing; it is not life. To be worn down by the storm of a thousand years is a tedious death at best. I do not want to be a thing of stone any longer. And it is very cruel to have such heavy wings. As if flight were even possible with these mockeries," the creature remarked. "When the rays from the star come this Christmas Eve, I will not seek refuge beneath the old bells of the village square. I will allow myself to become a man."

News of the gargoyle's decision spread throughout the island.

One witch in particular was most surprised. Witches are generally not afraid of or at odds with the gargoyles, and in fact appreciate them for their decorative flair.

The witch flew down to the top of the broken castle that the gargoyle sat upon to speak with the gargoyle about his decision.

"Why are you doing this?" asked the witch. "If you wished, I could turn you into something other than you are. I could transform you into a giant golem made of clay. That way you could mold yourself into whatever you wanted, on whatever days you wanted. Your tedium would end. And you would not have to worry about being eaten or being turned into a vampire by the others."

The gargoyle thought for a time. "Yes, but your spells do not last for all time, and I would become a gargoyle again."

"But you could die. Once the transformation is complete, you will be prey for all the other monsters here. Humanity will be known for only moments."

The gargoyle hadn't thought about this. "But, think of what you might have become if you had remained human? Wouldn't you just once like to touch your feet to the ground and feel the soil between your toes?"

"Witches don't have toes."

"Not anymore," he said slowly. "You don't need them now that you build your huts on sticks and poles and no longer trust the Earth. Do you know what gargoyles do? We sit and watch. We sit and watch everything. We watch the wolves that were men hunt and feed on each other. We watch as you witches trade your souls and your beauty for trinkets and petty incantations. We watch Moth Men devour the cloth ragamuffins only to be charred by the volcano giants. This is an island of trivial war. Nothing is solved by these violent and bloody engagements, nothing at all. And I am so very tired of watching nothing and gaining nothing in my observation of these events."

"It is better here than in the world of men. They fight for nothing as well. At least here we have power." The witch nodded to herself. She knew she was right.

"Do we? We're all we can ever be here. If we die here, we become ghosts of the monsters we were. Is that power? In the world of men, though similar wars are fought, change is possible almost daily. Sometimes their wars do indeed purchase peace for a time. Sometimes their sacrifices make a difference and inspire each other. No, we have no power here, because we cannot change ourselves. I will do this thing, friend witch. I will become a man; the kind I could have been before I was bound to this enchantment. And I realize that after I have changed, I will not be able to call you 'friend witch' any longer. For then, I will be your prey."

"It does not have to be like this. Is the life of a monster so bad? You are one of the strongest and most powerful beings on the island. Why would you do this?"

"Peace on Earth. Good will towards men. Peace is for men, not for things like us. It's the promise of Christmas. And I am under its spell."

The witch was saddened at his use of the word 'spell', and even sadder yet at some of the other things the gargoyle had said. "I do not believe that I am trivial or that I am not still beautiful. There are some that find boils, growths and hunchbacks quite attractive. And to be toeless means that I don't have to scratch them as much as I would if I had them."

"Yes, friend witch, I am sure you are very attractive to some. And they all live on this island."

At that, the witch flew away, cursing the gargoyle. But of course, she knew her words had no effect, for how could words move a being of stone?

The gargoyle knew the witch was right. Once he became a man, he would most certainly be eaten or killed that Christmas Day. But at least he would see the dawn, when the star's light faded, and before the monsters emerged.

So he decided to approach each of the various races that lived on the island to decide which of them was most worthy of preying upon his humanity once the transformation was complete.

Gargoyles, being made of stone, cannot fly, but they can jump extremely long distances. This has, from time to time, given the impression of flight. And so, this gargoyle began his search for a worthy monster to take his life.

When the gargoyle landed amongst the werewolves, they howled and tried to scratch him. But their claws broke on his stone skin.

"Perhaps you will get to me first. That would be a good death. I would only ask that you do more than scratch me. I do not want to become one of your number. I want to die a man."

The wolves howled their approval and stood up on their hind legs as if to salute the old gargoyle. For a moment, there was something almost man-like that the gargoyle could see in them; a sense of mercy and acknowledgement and respect. But it was gone too quickly. There were no promises, only the chance, that if the wolves got to him first, he might not survive to become like them.

Once again the gargoyle took to the skies above the island in a giant leap.

He landed in the midst of the vampires. They had been plotting what to do with him once he was a man and were very happy to see that he had come to them. Human blood, after all, was difficult to come by here.

"Ah, Gargoyle. We are glad you have come," one of them hissed. "We would like to invite you to stay in our castle on Christmas Eve. We will have a feast, and have a great honor for you."

"I know why you want me. You want my blood. And if I am here when the star's rays no longer touch your castle, I will be easy prey."

"There are no flies on you," said one of the other vampires.

"Not yet," the gargoyle responded. "But I am concerned that if I were to come here, you would only make me into a vampire as well. I do not want to be a monster anymore. Why, of all of the different races of creatures on the island, are you so intent on making me one of your species? You are the closest to humanity intellectually."

"We require numbers, Gargoyle. We are now only a very old family, but we should be far more than this. If we could reintroduce ourselves to the world as an island nation, human politics would recognize our numbers as something sovereign and worthy of respect and representation."

"But surely," remarked the gargoyle, "because you survive by feeding on them, they would make no such treaties or promises."

"You are wrong, stone one. They make treaties all the time with people who kill in the millions, and not for sustenance, either. Once a treaty is written, we believe many of them will come to us, if only to be fed upon and become like us, living forever. We do not understand why you are so tempted by mortality, when those you want to become like are so tempted by the prospect of what we can offer them."

"I have watched them as well," agreed the gargoyle. "And while you are correct about what tempts them, there is something about them. Something that if I could be that, even for a moment, it would make the difference in what I am forever."

"What is this thing?"

"I don't know. Potential, maybe? A chance to be something more. They are a mystery. There is more to them than we thought."

The vampires sneered at each other and made their Christmas Eve offer again.

The gargoyle merely shook his head and jumped away from them.

While the island is always in shadow, there is still a kind of 'day and night'. By day, the stars and the moon can be seen. By night, there is nothing but shadow. Even those dead worlds in the heavens that only reflect the light decline to offer anything to the island.

Night was coming and not just any night. It was Christmas Eve. The Christmas star would soon shine on him. And he would know what it was like to be a man.

The gargoyle was not sad that his life would soon be over

because he was not certain it truly would be. He was only sure that his life as a monster would come to an end. And this notion excited him to such a great degree that he considered ending his search and just allowing chance to determine his mortality.

He had time to visit one more race of creatures. He had not had time to visit them all. But it hardly mattered. How he died was less important than that he become fully human.

But his search had reminded him of something very important. Not all humans live as humans. Some live and breathe a sort of half-human existence, a lukewarm life at best.

Like the vampires, it is as if these people's waking hours were spent asleep, as if they moved through life without ever really tasting it.

The gargoyle, while committed to his course of action, did not want to become only partially human. He knew full well what that looked like. Before he came to the island, he had watched the lazy and those that lacked compassion for their fellow man. But his fellow monsters were wrong. Dead wrong—or more accurately undead wrong—but wrong nonetheless. There was more to humanity than its lowest common denominators.

He hit the water at such a speed that he created a wave that flooded the shore of the island. He had not come to see the creatures from the Black Sea, but rather to speak to the mermaids.

He sank to the bottom of the sea like a rock he was made of.

The mermaids swirled around him, looking at him with strange, gray eyes. Their hair flowed like seaweed and they spoke though a series of bubbles that passed through blue lips and popped on the skin of the gargoyle.

"Why have you come, creature of stone?"

"I want to know if you are ever sad."

"Why would you ask this?"

"Because you are two creatures in one. You are fish and you are women. Do you ever desire to be one or the other? The creatures from the Black Sea prefer women with legs. Are you bothered that they only see you as an enemy instead of something else?"

The mermaids were surprised at this question because they had fought the creatures of the Black Sea for so long, they themselves had indeed forgotten that they were women too.

"We were once sad as you say, Gargoyle, but have forgotten what it was to be one or the other."

"Do you want to remember?"

"We do not know. If we tried, we might become prey for those that come from the Black Sea. We cannot risk remembering in fear that it would make us vulnerable to our enemy."

"I see. Thank you," said the gargoyle. He leapt from the ocean floor, erupting from the sea before landing again on dry ground, back in the ruins.

Monsters all over the island were beginning to hide from the star that began to show itself over the horizon. Its rays beat down upon the island, exposing every shadow and highlighting every ruin.

The zombies lumbered around him, not even conscious of the gargoyle. Of all the races of monsters that inhabited the island, they alone would be unchanged by the star's rays. They were beyond the ability to be changed by even something as potent as Christmas.

"I am only a thing of stone," said the gargoyle to one of the zombies. "You are denser still. Goodbye."

The gargoyle stood there at last, and let the rays touch him. At first his stone skin began to grow hot and red. Then it began to chip in places and even to blister. He had not expected to feel pain. He had, after all, not felt pain for a very long time. He felt tempted to seek the refuge of the old bell.

And then he looked at his hands. Light was now coming out of his fingers and shining back into his face. His stone body began to crack and melt and splinter all at the same time. It was like an earthquake had begun within the fault lines of his very body. He fell to the ground, shaking. But he did not cry out for help. No creature would come if he did. And he wanted this. He wanted to feel.

He spent the entire night, which felt like a lifetime, beingr remade by the rays of the star.

When at last the star's rays began to fade, he found that the light that came from his fingers had not stopped shining. And his wings, which had been heavy stone, had become something almost silken and as light as gossamer.

The gargoyle was a being of light now. He was like a god, not like a man at all. He had been completely transformed. And everything around him became shadow compared to him. If any human being were to see him now, that man or woman or child would have no reasonable response other than to bow down and worship him.

His eyes were like suns. He could see the monsters through the stone and trees and rock, hiding from him as if he himself were now like the star of Christmas.

He now realized that men were only creatures in transformation as well, caught in a place between gods and monsters. Humanity was a sort of chrysalis stage, not an end at all. To be human was to be like a steppingstone leading to another shore.

This angel, if such a word is proper to describe the creature that had once been a gargoyle, wanted to transform the other monsters of the island but he could do nothing; he was powerless to do so.

For they preferred to remain monsters, hiding from Christmas and all that it might make of them. And Christmas cannot be forced on anyone.

# PEACE UNDER EARTH

"He's dead."

The coroner spoke those very words. I heard him saying them. I heard him. And what was so terrible was that I am the man he was speaking of.

But I'm not dead. I'm alive.

I'm alive.

I'm alive.

I'm alive.

This is all a mistake, a terrible mistake because I'm not dead. Do you hear me? I'm not dead, you stupid doctor. I'm alive. What's wrong with you? I promise I won't sue. Just open your eyes.

I tried to scream, to beg him to look closer. But I couldn't move a muscle in my body. I couldn't even blink or cry. It was paralysis on a level unlike any I would have imagined possible.

The coroner closed my eyelids.

Everything was black.

I would be buried alive the next day, and I couldn't lift a finger to stop it.

The next morning, I felt myself being carried somewhere; into another room, I think, or maybe out to a car. Then I was lowered into what I assume was a casket...and not a nice one, either. This was wood. The casket was then driven somewhere. I was tossed around within the confines of the casket. There were many hills, many ditches. If I were now going to be buried, it would not be in a conventional graveyard. They were taking me somewhere else. Finally, the ride ended and I felt myself being carried again.

I heard some words being spoken and the sounds of some rattles. I heard a chicken. Was I on a farm? And then the clucking was gone. Something dropped on the lid of the casket, something liquid spattering. The casket and I were lowered down into the ground. I could hear some voices say "bell maker" and some other words I could not make out. And then the dirt began dropping on the casket lid above my head. The voices became muffled and finally I couldn't hear them at all.

I was being buried at this moment. And despite everything my mother had ever told me, I was not late for my own funeral; I was early.

This was some sort of voodoo ritual. This was no mistake. I had been cursed. It was a woman's voice I'd heard. But I'm not the bell maker. It was just a joke. Please.

Of course, no words came from my lips. There was nothing I could say to defend myself.

I'm here, buried alive, because of a favor I did for a friend. This guy I know makes bells. These are not little bells, either. I'm talking about giant the-hunchback-still-has-job-security kind of bells. I've seen Adam's workshop. Each one must weigh at least a ton.

He knew my family was here in New Orleans and he knew I'd be down here for the holidays, so he asked me to video tape his bell being rung for the first time at a Christmas Eve Mass at Saint Thomas's Cathedral.

Everyone in the city turned out for this thing. It's not just a part of a church; it's like a major addition to the city landscape.

I went to a party after and thought it would be cool to act like I was the one that made the bell. Everyone was talking about it, about the purity of the ringing. One woman said the sound was so pure, so perfect, that she was going to go to church again, that she had forgotten how things could be. She kissed me because she thought I was you, Adam. It was a good kiss. Like a strawberry.

I met this homeless guy who kept on thanking me over and over for what I'd done. He claimed that he couldn't remember the last three years of his life. But he heard the bell, and it woke him from…what did he call it…? Oh, yeah; he called it 'dead awake'. I told him it would probably be better if he didn't drink anymore.

And then this other guy asked me if I was the bell maker. I nodded. The guy gave me a really strong drink and the next thing I know is I'm looking up at a doctor who's pronouncing me dead.

This has something to do with voodoo, I'm certain of it. But I don't know why. All I know is that I'm not dead, but I soon will be.

Maybe I'm dying now because I lied and said I was the bell maker. Maybe they hate bell makers down here. So, Adam, wherever you are this Christmas, I hope you appreciate this, man.

I'm generally late for everything. Story of my life. I suppose that what I've been told is true; it's a power play, a way to make certain that life does not go on without me.

Well, life's going on without me now.

If these are my last moments, I suppose I should try to do something. But I can't call for help. I can't scream. I can't move a muscle.

I will probably go mad here, or suffocate. If that's the case, I suppose I should use this time to do some serious thinking about my life. And maybe even pray the prayers that I had never dared to before, even if it's just to myself. If there is a God, does he hear the things we can't or don't say?

I guess I'm sorry that I haven't been more significant to anybody. I mean, I manage a bookstore, but it's not like my own words have meant anything to anyone. I want to think I have, or at least, had something to say to people. Maybe about life, or how to live it.

That sounds so stupid.

I come home twice a year to pretend I'm committed to my family and my parents. But am I? We have the same conversations, the same arguments, tell the same jokes. Give the same kind of gifts. Get the same kinds of socks. Smile and say thank you.

Every Christmas is the same. We have the same conversations, the same hopes for a better year next year. We speak the same apologies. It's almost like going to mass. As if the words repeated over and over again will become more meaningful the more often they are spoken.

Maybe there is some sort of significance in that. Maybe there is a comfort in the idea that whatever changes happen in the world, family remains. The words stay the same.

But here, now, six feet under, I don't know.

This is definitely not the way to die. To lie here, regretting and wanting to change everything. Wanting my life to mean something to somebody.

All because I wanted some credit, even if I didn't deserve it.

Sorry Adam. You made the bell. You made the difference in these people's lives down here. I didn't.

But I took all the congratulations for the bell.

I took the kiss meant for you.

I took the thanks from the guy with the memory loss.

I took the drink from…the drink…it was the drink. That strong drink…that's what did this. Maybe it was a drug or something.

Maybe…it will wear off. Maybe I'll be able to move again soon. And then I'll be able to…to…

Where will I go?

I'll be able to move only so that I can scream and tear my fingers to the bone while I try to climb out.

No.

I'm not going to die that way.

I will lie here, and I will wait for death. And when it comes, despite all my wasted opportunities, I will greet it knowing that at least I finished this well. At least I did it without freaking out.

Here I am.

Dead awake.

Sorry I can't kneel, God.

I'm sorry that you and I really haven't talked that much over the years. I'm sure we'll be able to make up for that in the years to come. I've just been really busy.

I hear you're very understanding and very forgiving, so I think that if you really did make this world, and fill it with all the things you have, well, that you'd understand. And you won't judge me too harshly for why I wasn't all I could be here, there was just so much to do, or at least, so much to distract me from caring for people. I'm sorry.

I want you to know that I don't blame you for this. I went to a party instead of spending time with my family. It was my choice. I chose my career. I chose my friends. I chose to take credit for something that wasn't mine.

Thank you for my life.

It wasn't all a waste.

Please God, give me peace.

I had been right about the drink being a drug. Because although all I saw was black, I became aware that my eyes were now open. I could feel the tears running down the side of my cheek. I was conscious that although I had very little space to move, I could.

I thought about screaming, of crying out, of scratching at the sides and top of the casket, but I knew it would be in vain, like so much of my life.

No. It was okay, now.

So this is peace.

I fell asleep.

And dreamed such amazing dreams about my family and about what they could still be to me. I dreamed about the conversations we had together, about saying the words we always said to each other, but they were different now, they were deeper, I heard them now in ways I never had before. They were all I could hope for. And in my dream, I prayed again, even harder. This time, I prayed that I would never wake up. That I would stay here with my family during the holidays forever. I prayed harder this time, that I would never wake up again...

⚬⚬⚬⚬⚬

**B**ut this prayer was not answered.
I woke to hear a terrible scratching above my head and was suddenly flooded by a terrible light.

I was dug out of this grave by the man I met at the party; the one who told me that he had been 'dead awake'.

I learned that your bell, Adam, was just that good. A local voodoo priestess had lost her hold on her...well, I guess you'd call them zombies. But when your bell rang on that Christmas Eve, so many people were freed from her domination. You saved them, Adam. You did.

She was so angry that she ordered her few remaining followers to bury the bell maker alive.

But one of those you saved, saved me.

For him, it was your bell that woke him.

For me, it was being buried alive. I had not realized how dead I was.

When I arrived home later that Christmas day, and saw my parents and brothers and sisters, I entered with my usual "Sorry I'm late."

No one seemed to notice. They expected it and continued whatever they had been doing.

But they stopped the moment I said, "It won't happen again."

# THE GHOST OF CHRISTMAS PRESENTS

The toy-maker's name was Thomas. There was no better toy-maker in all the land and there were no better toys to be found anywhere.

Thomas almost always had a smile on his face, especially when he was around other people. He would never frown in front of the town's children, even if he were sad. It was a matter of pride. It was an issue of principle. And perhaps that is why he was so loved by the children. They knew they were safe with him.

The reason he was sad at times had less to do with circumstance and far more with a feeling that he didn't quite belong in this town of his. He felt…well, like a fish out of water. Like he was not really a citizen of the town, but a citizen of a different town entirely. He couldn't remember where. He could not even remember quite how he came to this town. Perhaps this was to be expected. He was, after all, quite old.

But, under no circumstances would he ever let others see his discontent, and worked only to add to their happiness.

Even his critics knew that his toys were the finest anywhere. Everyone knew this. What was most amazing was the fact that his toys did not break. They would literally last a lifetime and beyond.

They could be played with forever, he'd say. The toys would never wear down, never tarnish, and they would never ever crack— though the same could not be said for the children Thomas made the toys for.

Or the world he lived in.

T ime marches on. But unlike one of Thomas's tin soldiers, time moves whether we wind it or not. It never stops. It never gives up. And we are all like breakable toys in its clumsy fingers.

War raged around the borders of the small town that was called Gutenberg. Because they were hidden in the mountains, the people were confident that they would never be found by the enemy. They thought they were safe.

Still, there is nothing like a war to take the joy and fun out of Christmas, and toy-making.

Everyone experiences war on different levels. Everyone feels the pain of war in different ways. The men who fought the war had once been boys who played at fighting. Thomas may have even made the metal soldiers that some of them once played with. He made the toy guns. He made the mock armor. He made the toy tanks. In many ways, he was their first general.

But the glory and the fun of all those wars were now replaced by a new battle, a terrible and fearsome one. And the fighting was no longer between friends and brothers; it was between killers and strangers.

Many of the boys Thomas had made toys for had returned from the war to Gutenberg.

Some returned, but with broken and missing pieces. Some came back in caskets.

The town mourned the loss of their children. They wept over the deaths of their good young men and women until their tears became rusty and the crying no longer brought a sense of release. Perhaps they mourned too long. Perhaps the luxury of being hidden and not having to be concerned with the war around them did not keep them safe, but instead was a danger in and of itself.

Of all the people in the town, Thomas alone questioned their safety. He wondered and speculated what would happen if the town and its people were discovered by the enemy. And so, he began to devise an escape plan. The few he initially spoke to, including the mayor, rebuked him for trying to start a conspiracy against the town itself.

But Thomas feared that he was a man living amongst ostriches.

Any time he spoke to adults about the subject, they ignored him and told him be quiet.

Thomas often imagined them all sticking their heads in the dirt and ignoring the danger that was out there.

But when Thomas spoke to the children, he learned that the children were afraid. The promises of safety from their parents did not help them with their nightmares, did not ease their fears of dying.

And so, Thomas shared his idea with them. The idea was that the children would hide in the caves beneath the mountains. Thomas knew of a cave, a special cave that would take them all to safety should the town come under attack.

Thomas knew that the journey to the cave was long and hard. It was difficult. And so the children would not be able to carry much with them.

So Thomas built the most miraculous of toys for the children. They were no larger than the palm of a child's hand and could fit easily into a child's pocket. There were teddy bears, and trains, and balls, and dolls and almost any other toy you could imagine, on the tiniest of scales. And, these were toys made by Thomas, so they lost none of their detail or design.

But as amazing as these toys looked, their small size and almost weightless nature was not the miracle.

The miracle was that when a child played with one of them, when they held the toy in their hand, they felt like they were playing with a regular sized toy. Holding the tiny bear to their cheek felt like they were hugging a giant teddy. Pushing the mini-train along the ground gave the child the feeling that they were forging ahead with a giant toy locomotive.

The children were overjoyed. But Thomas warned them not to tell their parents about the toys, to keep them to themselves. And of course, the children were not to speak of the cave or the escape plan.

Thomas knew that should the enemy attack, the adults, caught off guard, would certainly follow them all to the cave.

The children all promised and continued with their preparations to leave. But joy and happiness and a new absence of fear are difficult things to contain. Nor is it a good thing to keep to oneself in most circumstances. And eventually the adults in the town discovered what Thomas had done and the plan he had made.

The adults of Gutenberg were overwhelmed with anger. Who was Thomas to suggest they could not keep their children safe? Who was Thomas to plan for an escape? He was a toy-maker. And for that matter, of what use were toys in a time of war?

The adults were reminded of something inside of them that had been taken away by this war. Those adults, those grown men and women who had once been parents, could have been helped and healed by the children's joy and love for Thomas' toys. But they were not. They were reminded only of what they'd lost, of what had been taken from them. They had failed to keep their grown children safe, and now Thomas was suggesting—in the form of an escape plan—that their very homes were no longer havens.

Perhaps it should not come as a surprise then that the town itself became embittered with Thomas' involvement in the children's lives.

Thomas tried to explain that the plans were just in the case of an enemy attack; that these, like his toys, were not only for the children. They were for everyone.

The town closed Thomas' workshop that very day. Of course, the children did their best to keep the small toys Thomas had made for them in secret.

The adults sneered at and reviled Thomas. They resented him for making the toys for children. They hated him because they took the toys away from the children.

Now it would be very easy to hate these townspeople, but it is also important to remember that they had once been very loving parents. They had once loved Thomas and his toys. But they had lost so much. And like their children—at least, the ones who had made it back from the war—there were parts of them that been broken too.

They hated Thomas because he still had what they did not…the love of the children.

So, although what they did next was terrible, remember that no one sets out in life to be cruel. No one desires to smash or break.

All the adults—especially those who had once been parents—built a fire in the center of the village. It was a giant fire piled high with the things of childhood. Cribs, playpens, highchairs—anything that would remind them that they were ever parents at all—was placed on this fire.

And they swept through their attics and their basements, searching for Thomas' toys. Every single toy in the city was placed on that fire. Every single item that was loved by a child, except for the miraculous palm-sized toys Thomas had just built, was cast into the flames that shot high into the night air.

The mob tore down Thomas' workshop, burning it as well. The flames danced higher and higher in the air until finally they began to falter and fall, exhausted by their own ferocity.

When at last, there was little more than smoke left, the adults in the village were overcome with the terror of seeing that none of the toys had been burned in the fire. Nor were they hot to the touch.

Thomas smiled a small, shameful but surprisingly defiant smile. "Old-world craftsmanship. I don't cut corners."

"Indeed," said the Burgermeister of the town. "Your toys mock our pain and loss, old man. Who are you to curse us so? Who are you to cause so much pain?"

"But I am only a toy-maker. I help children," Thomas said. "What could be wrong with that? It would be my shame to build anything that wasn't for the children."

"It is wrong that anything should last like your toys do. It is wrong that they should outlive us."

"It is wrong," said Thomas, "that you should deny your children the joy they might experience because of your own pain. Children don't want toys that break."

The adults stared at Thomas. How could he be so cold to them in light of their pain? How could he continue to do what he did? Did he not see their loss? Did he not understand what had happened to them?

They could not bear the sight of him. And so they did something awful. But perhaps, in the end, it was for the best.

The townsfolk turned on Thomas. They grabbed his toys and began to throw them at him. Trains were used like clubs and flails. Jumping ropes became whips. The strings of the puppets became nooses.

The children just stared in horror.

Thomas looked up at them and smiled even then, one last time. "Go. Run. The enemy is already here. You know the plan."

The children did run that day. They ran with the miracles Thomas had made for them in their pockets. They ran to the cave in the mountains. They ran to where they would finally be utterly safe.

After the children had gone, soldiers entered the town. The war had indeed come to Gutenberg. The commander of this enemy division had seen the fire that had been built. It gave away the town's location.

Thomas' toys survived the enemy's guns and tanks and soldiers. The same cannot be said of the residents of Gutenberg.

The commander and his men were surprised that in a town with so many toys, no children were found.

He was even more perplexed that there was a toy in the dead hand of every man and woman in Gutenberg.

As for Thomas, his story was far from over. For Thomas, who had never felt like much of a part of the city of Gutenberg, found himself feeling very much like he was at home in the giant city he woke up in.

There were children everywhere and they were all calling him by name and thanking him for coming back to them.

This was no small town he was now in, but a sprawling and

majestic metropolis. It was a place of vast forests and parks and steel mills, of metal girders and workshops and skyscrapers and gondolas. It was an amazing place indeed.

The governor of the province visited the day Thomas awoke and told him how happy he was that Thomas had returned.

"Thank you, sir," said Thomas, not yet understanding where he was. "I'm not certain why everyone says I have returned. What is this place? It feels like home. I feel like I belong here, but I cannot remember. Did the children escape? Did we…"

"I don't want to seem authoritarian, Thomas, but we must make certain this does not happen again. It is not good to wander through the fogs and the caves outside the city."

"What?"

"City limits. You need to stay here. You can't go leaving for down there again."

"Down where?"

"Amongst the living." The governor realized he needed to explain himself.

"The living?" asked Thomas, as the reality of who and what he had become began to dawn on him.

"Yes, Thomas. Your gifts are for those children that find themselves here. They will be children forever in this place, and require toys for the long journey ahead."

Thomas smiled. He had been correct all the time. He didn't belong in Gutenberg. Was he a ghost? Or something else? And what was this city?

He shrugged off the questions. He smiled even more broadly. How important could the answers really be? He thought about the children and began to build again, knowing that the toys he made hereafter would be played with forever.

# EVIL ELF

When an elf is wished into being, it has a destiny. Many elves, as you may guess, are destined to become toy-makers. Within the very old and highly-respected tradition of toy-making elves, there are a variety of opportunities to find fulfillment in Santa's employ.

But there are some elves who are not destined to be toy-makers. Some elves find themselves working in the stables, grooming and preparing Santa's reindeer for their Christmas Eve run. Still other elves guard the location of Santa's mansion and toy factory at the North Pole.

But one elf in particular had a different calling altogether. At least, that's what he told himself.

He could have been called Flim. That would have been a good elvish name. In the years that followed, he thought of all the great names he could have had instead. He'd try these names on for size like a pair of pointy-toed socks.

The custom at the North Pole is this. After an elf is hatched, it is brought before Santa's wizard to determine the elf's destiny; after which, the elf is named.

But there were complications for the elf that might have been named Flim. For when Could-Have-Been-Flim was brought to the magic ice-caves to have his destiny revealed and have his name chosen, something terrible happened. The ice mirrors turned black.

The wizard whispered in Santa's ear. And just so there is no confusion, this is Santa Claus, old Kris Kringle himself.

Santa, who had been up until that moment overwhelmingly jolly, began to cough. He coughed and shook so loudly and violently that a number of the magic ice mirrors shattered.

He continued to cough for so long that he was given immediate bed rest and spent six months under the care and supervision of Mrs. Claus and those elves born to ensure Santa's comfort and personal health.

Neither the wizard nor Santa ever revealed what was discovered about the elf.

Everyone at the North Pole knew something was wrong. For Santa was never quite the same after that. Yes, he still gave gifts. Certainly, he continued to try to be merry, he still ate cookies by the billions every year, and he never stopped serving Christmas in the ways he knew. But somehow, his merriment was no longer all it had been. Some of the joy had been taken out of his ho-ho-ho.

As for the elf who could have been Flim, he was not named that day. Santa's collapse had interrupted the proceedings.

Might-Be-Flim was named by the other elves, instead.

He was called Evil.

And oh, how he hated that name.

Almost as much as he hated them for giving him that name.

It's difficult being called Evil. And it's difficult being around someone who's called Evil. No one would argue this.

Evil didn't spend much time with the other elves. He hid and lived alone in the caves surrounding the toy factory and chalet.

Sometimes he'd smell something good on the winds and know that the elves were making cookies to keep Santa happy…well, satisfied, at least…until Christmas came.

Interesting sidenote; elves are known for making cookies, but they never make crackers. That's just a myth.

Evil even ventured towards the kitchens a few times to try to get a cookie for himself, but the looks and whispers of all who saw him were too much for his already-ridiculed heart.

So he'd just return to the caves where he would eat frost

mushrooms…which I'm certain you will be unsurprised to hear don't taste nearly as good as cookies.

And Evil would have remained there in the caves, unseen by all who served Christmas for the rest of his life…had it not been for the garbage that blew into his cave one day.

It was far more than a scrap of paper. It was The List.

No, it was not The Good List. This was the other one, the list that had all the names of the bad kids on it. It was a long, long list.

All the names of all the kids that were deemed…well, *evil*…were on this list.

And they *were* evil.

The elf looked at the list. He thought about these children who spoke back to their parents, who were jealous of their brothers and sisters, who were very sad before they ever did anything bad, and he wondered about himself.

He was not as alone as he had originally supposed. There were lots of evils in the world. He was only one of them.

Evil began traveling around the world, visiting these children that had been condemned to getting no presents from Santa just for pulling their sister's hair, or for not understanding the delicate needs of the family pets. He watched these kids.

He saw them cry. He saw them pout. And he watched them pretend to sleep, listening while their parents complained to each other about how difficult having children like them was.

The more Evil saw, the angrier he became.

And soon—which was actually about ten years, but still soon to someone who lives forever—the elf called Evil came up with a plan.

He decided to steal all of Santa's best gifts and give them to the bad kids, the Naughty Listers. Evil wasn't welcome among the elves, but among these kids, he'd be their Santa.

This would show that goody-goody Santa. This would show the other elves. This would show those parents that spoke of their children as evil. The elf even laughed, thinking that when the good kids saw what the evil ones got this year, there'd be a mass conversion.

Santa's Naughty List was about to get a whole lot longer.

Evil smiled and schemed.

Now, in the history of the North Pole and Santa's workshop, stables and factory, there has never been a theft. There has never been any crime. And that is why elves are never born for law-enforcement purposes. And that is also why, when all the elves were sleeping that snowy December 23rd, it was so easy for Evil to sneak in, steal so many of the very best toys and begin to carry out his plan.

He took one of Santa's old sleighs, which was more like a hot-air balloon and did not require reindeer. This is because he did not expect to find any reindeer that would be sympathetic to his plan.

Evil hid the toys in the caves until the next night.

Of course, Santa searched everywhere the next day for the toys meant for the very best of children. He was so frustrated in fact that he called for the wizard again to help him find these fantastic toys.

Evil watched from a distance as Santa entered the wizard's magic ice caves. The elf called Evil had forgotten about the wizard and his magic ice mirrors. The plan was not going to work. Surely the wizard's mirrors would reveal where the toys were hidden.

Evil did not know what to do. He paced back and forth though the cave. Should he sneak the toys back? No, it was too late for that. Should he risk a daylight departure? No, they'd see him then. And Santa would certainly stop him. Evil had been thwarted.

But, when Santa stepped out of the wizard's cave moments later, he did not race to Evil's lair. No, the wizard accompanied an obviously upset Santa back to his factory, even allowing Santa to lean on him for part of the walk back.

There, Santa prepared for his Christmas Eve rounds without bothering to look for the stolen Christmas toys again.

Evil the elf came up with two theories about this. Maybe the ice mirrors had failed to reveal where the elf and stolen toys were. Or, even better, maybe the wizard hadn't told Santa where he was. That would mean that the wizard was in favor of Evil's plan. That would make him an evil wizard.

The elf was overjoyed at this thought. And so he prepared his balloon sleigh and the toys for that night's trip.

There were at least three occasions during the evening that Evil could have sworn his path crossed with Santa and his flying sleigh. Evil would try to maneuver his balloon into the clouds. He'd do everything he could. Still, he wondered, how could it be that Santa missed him?

But if Santa did see Evil that evening, he did nothing about it, for Evil returned to the North Pole later that morning, having distributed Santa's best to all those considered the worst.

Evil was just about to sleep in his cave when he became aware of the wizard's presence.

"Your evening's work is finished?" asked the wizard in a way that seemed less like a question and more like a statement.

Evil stood up from where he had settled. "You *did* know. I knew it. You *are* an evil wizard!"

"Come with me," said the wizard, and he took Evil to the cave of the magic ice mirrors.

Evil stood in the middle of a great hall surrounded by reflections of the world around them. It was Christmas morning and the children Evil had given toys to were now waking.

To say that these children's parents were surprised to find elf-made gifts for their kids is to miss the point.

These children, the very kids that knew they were evil, saw, at last, that they had not been forgotten. That they had not been ignored.

Now, in all Evil's journeys, he never bothered to leave a note saying these glorious toys were not from Santa, so the children just assumed they were.

The elf called Evil was surprised to see these children begin to cry. But these were not the tears of children who were selfish. These were the tears of children who realized they had not been forgotten; they had not been passed over.

Christmas had not left them alone.

And as the mirrors began to do their magic, the destinies of these children began to change. Once, these evil children would have grown to do more evil in the world. But now, Evil watched as many of them grew up to do great good and greater acts of courage and hope.

And those children that had been good, and had received second tier toys that year, were happy with what they received that morning. They were not angry. They did not feel cheated. In fact, they were happy to see brothers and sisters, who had always been so nasty to them, become kinder.

The elf called Evil saw that he had not succeeded in making the Naughty List grow longer, but had made it disappear almost entirely.

Evil was dizzy, spinning around the hall, from mirror to mirror, seeing one child after another change into something and someone new.

He stopped looking in the mirrors when he realized Santa was standing before him.

"I am sorry, elf-with-no-name," said Santa.

"They call me Evil," said the elf.

"I know," said Santa, who seemed sad with a sort of understanding. "I want you to know how sorry I am."

"*You're* sorry?" asked the elf. "But why? I stole your best toys. I took your balloon sleigh. I made you sick for over a year. I stole the joy from your ho-ho-ho."

Santa began to laugh in that moment. It was a deep, rich laugh, one that no elf had ever heard before. It made Santa's customary ho-ho-ho seem like a polite chuckle by comparison.

This made the elf called Evil more than a little frightened.

Santa continued. "I am sorry for so many things. I am sorry you've had to go so long without your true name. I am sorry they called you Evil. I am sorry for what you've had to go through."

The elf, of course, did not understand.

The wizard nodded and all the ice mirrors reflected the day the elf was hatched, those many years before. The elf watched the wizard in the mirror whisper into Santa's ear. He heard the words the wizard had spoken that had made Santa so sick.

"This nameless elf will help you remember all you've forgotten, Santa Claus. For you no longer know Christmas at all. You will weep one day for the evil you have caused."

The elf looked away from the reflections of the past and at Santa in the here and now, who was laughing still.

"I don't understand," said the elf. "And Santa's not weeping."

The wizard smiled. "He is, brave elf. He cries even now. But not all his tears are the result of evil he's committed; some are in the recognition of good. These are the proper tears before Christmas."

The elf hated the way the wizard and Santa were talking. He hated the mysteries behind their words. The wizard continued anyway.

"Sometimes elves cannot be named until they become what they were meant to become. And if you had known then what was to happen, you would never have reached this moment. Sometimes the evils done to us are really very good things indeed. And the names given intended to harm, do the greatest good imaginable."

"What are you talking about? I'm Evil. I stole toys. I gave to bad kids. I did this to make more kids evil, and you're calling me brave?"

Santa stopped laughing and crying. He knelt down in front of the elf and looked in his eyes.

"Thinking Christmas is only for the good," Santa replied, "was probably the greatest evil of all. I had forgotten that Christmas was also for those who deserved it the least. I had forgotten that Christmas was meant to banish the lists of the wicked forever."

The elf that had been called Evil was dumbstruck. "You're not going to tell me I saved Christmas, are you?"

"No," laughed Santa again. "You saved all those that I would have missed. And you saved me."

The elf that had been called Evil was given a new name, of course, and one that was impossible to spell. But his name would be regarded as blessed in the highest courts of Christmas for all time. And whatever it is that comes after that.

Of course, this upset the elf more than ever. So he left the factory and Santa's workshop, swearing never to return, and well, just swearing. It was difficult to wipe and knock the snow from his feet as he left, because there was snow wherever he went.

This only added to his frustration, of course.

He eventually settled down and made his home in a cave atop a mountain a few hundred miles south of the North Pole.

No longer surviving on elf food, whether it be stolen cookie crumbs or frost mushrooms, he was amazed to find that he eventually grew taller, but was never able to get rid of his elvish pot-belly.

His pointy-toed socks inside his pointy-toed shoes, though, much to his irritation, were a bit tighter than usual, but hardly the sole reason for his disposition.

If the memory of what he had done and what had happened wasn't enough, he now had neighbors down in the valley beneath the mountain to contend with. He especially hated their parties and singing.

They didn't call him Evil. They had a different name. But it meant the same thing. Who were they to name him? Who?

They liked to say that the day this lanky elf came to make his home above them, well, that his heart shrank three sizes that day.

How could they possibly know, of course, that it had happened well before he settled on Mount Crumpit?

# Biographies

## (in order of appearance)

**Cover Artist/Internal Art, JOHN K. SNYDER III**

John K. Snyder III is an Eisner-nominated Illustrator and writer of comic books and graphic novels. Creator of the independent comic series *Fashion In Action*, and adapter/illustrator of the graphic novel adaptation of Grand Master mystery writer Lawrence Block's classic novel *Eight Million Ways to Die*, published by IDW. He has worked for nearly every major publisher, including DC, Dark Horse, Marvel, IDW, and many others. Snyder worked on *Suicide Squad* during its classic 1980's run with writers John Ostrander and Kim Yale, and provided covers for the 2007 Suicide Squad mini-series and Suicide Squad covers coinciding with the release of the 2021 James Gunn movie. Along with Matt Wagner, Snyder co-created the Pieter Cross version of *Doctor Mid-Nite* for DC and *Lady Zorro* for Dynamite. Snyder also worked with Wagner on the epic *Grendel: God and the Devil* storyline. John has also illustrated covers for author Jim Krueger's renowned *Foot Soldiers* comics series and is delighted to be working with Jim once again on this book. Find him at http://www.johnksnyder.com and as @johnksnyder3 on Instagram and Threads, @JohnKSnyderIII1 on Twitter, and John K Snyder III on Facebook.

**Introduction Writer, JONATHAN MABERRY**

Jonathan Maberry is a *NYTimes* bestselling author, #1 Audible bestseller, 5-time Bram Stoker Award-winner, 4-time Scribe Award winner, Inkpot Award winner, comic book writer, and producer. He is the author of 51 novels, 16 short story collections, 28 graphic novels, 170 short stories, 14 nonfiction books, and has edited 26 anthologies. He has written comics for Marvel, IDW, Dark Horse, and others, and *Black Panther: Wakanda Forever* is based in part on his 2009-10 run on the comic. His Joe Ledger thrillers are being developed for TV by the director of the John Wick films. He is the president of the International Association of Media Tie-in Writers, and editor of *Weird Tales* Magazine. Find him at www.jonathanmaberry.com and as @jonathanmaberry on Twitter, Instagram, and Threads.

## Author, JIM KRUEGER

Jim Krueger is the former Creative Director of Marvel Comics and a *New York Times* best-selling author, best-known for his work on iconic comic book titles such as *Earth X, Justice, Avengers, Star Wars* and more. He has written for some of the biggest publishers in the business, and collaborated with industry heavyweights like Alex Ross, Gerard Way, Sam Raimi, Bill Sienkiewicz and John Paul Leon. In addition to his work in comics, Jim has written for film, television, and video games, contributing to projects such as the *Spider-Man 2* video game, *Mortal Combat* and the animated series *Justice League,* among others. A visionary creator, Jim's ideas about world-building have been a major influence in shaping popular culture through comics, TV, and film. His groundbreaking *Earth X* trilogy, which was awarded Best Series of the Year by *Wizard Magazine,* became the basis for much of the Marvel Universe continuity, influencing movies and TV shows such as *Black Panther, Eternals, Moon Knight, Captain Marvel,* and *Loki.*